Hired Hand

Hired Hand

Nelson Nye

THORNDIKE
CHIVERS

This Large Print edition is published by Thorndike Press®, Waterville, Maine USA and by BBC Audiobooks Ltd, Bath, England.

Published in 2005 in the U.S. by arrangement with Golden West Literary Agency.

Published in 2006 in the U.K. by arrangement with Golden West Literary Agency.

U.S. Hardcover 0-7862-7923-0 (Western)
U.K. Hardcover 1-4056-3647-5 (Chivers Large Print)
U.K. Softcover 1-4056-3648-3 (Camden Large Print)

The text of this Large Print edition is unabridged.
Other aspects of the book may vary from the original edition.

Set in 16 pt. Plantin by Elena Picard.

Printed in the United States on permanent paper.

British Library Cataloguing-in-Publication Data available

Library of Congress Cataloging-in-Publication Data

Nye, Nelson C. (Nelson Coral), 1907–
    Hired hand / by Nelson Nye.
      p. cm. — (Thorndike Press large print westerns)
    ISBN 0-7862-7923-0 (lg. print : hc : alk. paper)
    1. Large type books. I. Title. II. Thorndike Press large print Western series.
PS3527.Y33H57 2005
  813′.54—dc22
                                   2005014749

Hired Hand

1

Mark Dawson, dropping his rump to the slick of the saddle, watched the van of the Muleshoe beef hit the stockyards. One more tough chore rolled under the bridge.

He pulled his glance away from the Alhambra. With six weeks of gruelling brush work behind him his throat felt dry as baled-up cotton. He slapped his quirt against a leather covered leg and loosened the gritty folds of his scarf.

The boys knew what to do. This herd wasn't going to get out of hand now. High Pockets and Kettlebelly, seen against gray rails through the billowing dust, were putting the steers up the chute like veterans. He'd have time for a shave and a soak in Ching's tub and then, after eating, he'd drop around and pick up that buyer's check.

He roved another look across the front of Quayle's saloon. Old Eph's son, Curly, was probably over there now, cutting the dust of the drive from his gullet. This reflection didn't help loosen Mark's muscles any and he kept whacking leather, stuck with the notion that an heir's predilections might assay considerable different if indulged by Eph's range boss.

Six months ago he would have laughed at such flapdoodle. He knew the Old Man would never open his mouth; yet he continued to sit, not willing even to himself to admit that he and Curly Thorpe were not as close as they had been.

"Hell, it's being away!" he told himself. "Man that's been off a range four years ain't likely to come back huggin' the things he took away with him!" Just the same there was a difference. It was a thorn digging into him whenever their eyes caught and locked.

They'd been brought up by Eph as brothers, sharing everything together, the wind, the sun, the stars, their frolics and their punishments, even batting their heads over the same identical problems until the Old Man had shipped Curly off to college. Actually, Mark was no relation to Eph's handsome son, just a parentless stray the Muleshoe owner had taken in after Apaches had got done playing hob with a wagon train. It hadn't bothered Mark that Eph had kept him here at the ranch; far from re-

8

senting Curly's education and prospects Mark had always felt an unquestioning gratitude and loyalty, proud of the work and long hours by which he'd earned his job as ramrod, proud to be known as Eph Thorpe's right hand.

He was a slow-talking man who had never got past the fifth grade in his schooling, a leather-legged galoot in flannel shirt and sweat-stained headgear. A mop of yellow hair tumbled over his weather-scrinched forehead. He had the short-nosed lumpy face that went with broad cheekbones and the build most generally associated with men who spent much time polishing the seat of a center-fire saddle. He had that kind of walk besides, and a reflective pair of turquoise eyes that could look twenty degrees colder than a well chain if you riled him — not that anyone often did.

He was considered by the outfit to be a pretty patient man. A shade on the serious side perhaps but easy-going, satisfied with small pleasures and content with his lot. His whole life, they would have told you, was wrapped up in Muleshoe. And so it was. He had never thought of himself in any other occupation.

In the lemon colored fog pawed up by the bawling beef Mark sat his big roan gelding hearing the voices of his men superimposed upon the clanking and chuff-chuffing of the wood-burning locomotive that was shunting the cars along the siding as the sweating cowhands filled them. They were loading the steers right into the cars, and as they were prodded up the chute the buyer and Lefty Red kept tally.

Mark was seeing these things but he wasn't really noticing. He was remembering how Curly had insisted on coming — "Getting back into harness" was the way Curly'd put it making his pitch before the Old Man. He'd been about as much help as a twenty-two cartridge in an eight-gauge shotgun and when he'd finally quit the herd about six miles back, two hours before daylight, everyone, Mark included, had heaved a heartfelt sigh of relief.

Now Mark picked up his reins and kneed his roan away from the cattle. There was a heap of rigs in town today. The whole main drag of Blossom, yonder, was stuffed and cluttered with them which — inasmuch as it wasn't payday — seemed uncommon odd until he noticed the big bunch of nesters standing and hunkered about the school-house yard. He remembered something then which old Eph and himself had let slip their minds in the press of this roundup and the excitement occasioned by Curly's return.

This was the day set aside by the county for the election of sheriff and other local officials and, if you could judge by that schoolyard, Journigan's weedbenders had turned out in full force.

Mark, scowling, swore softly under his breath. Terrapin and Jugwagon had their crews out on roundup and the polls would be closed before the boys got done with loading those cattle. He sent the roan toward the schoolhouse, looking for Joe Rainey.

Joe had been packing the tin as long as Mark could remember, a grizzled old-timer put in by the cow crowd and reelected last term despite the howls of the farmers Journigan's advertisements had fetched here. Joe had naturally done what he could to protect his backers and had held trouble down to a minimum. The truth was, of course, the big spreads' fences were illegal; only the water and a fraction of their holdings had been patented. The bulk of this range belonged to the government and had three years ago been thrown open to homesteading. Journigan, who, prior to that had been a small-spread owner, was now waxing fat on the fees he extracted for locating plow chasers.

11

Though a blustery sort he was possessed of much cunning and had taken full advantage of the discontent and unrest he had found among the haywire outfits — the "have-nots" as old Eph called them. It was a tribute to his dexterity that he had persuaded these spreads to throw in with the hoemen and gotten one of their number, Dink Fraesfield, to head the ticket opposing Joe Rainey.

Mark saw no sign of the sheriff when he stopped the roan beside a box elder thicket at the edge of the schoolyard. Several of the nesters turned their backs but the most of them kept staring with a thinly veiled hostility.

"Any of you boys seen the sheriff real recent?"

When it seemed as though no one was minded to answer, a dusty looking specimen in bib overalls asked truculently. "Which one?"

Mark's brows went up. "I was thinking of Joe Rainey."

The sodbuster nodded. "I reckoned you was." Swapping a glance with those nearest him the man in bib overalls scrinched his mouth and spat. Then, twisting around, he grinned up at Mark maliciously. "When they get done countin' the votes that old

12

buzzard'll be lucky if he don't get run outa town."

Mark let it pass, frowning down at his shadow, surprised to find the sun had bent it half across the yard. He kneed the big roan through silent clots of glowering nesters, pulling up wooden-cheeked before the schoolhouse steps.

He was about to toss down his reins and slide from leather when the door was slammed loudly. One of the group leaning against the building snickered.

"Looks," this man said, "like you're a little mite late."

Mark stared around him like a dog ringed by coyotes. That was how he felt; but in the interests of Muleshoe he only said mildly, "The polls don't close for another half hour yet."

"Must be somethin' wrong with your eyesight. They've done closed, mister," another man said.

Mark kept his mouth shut, knowing this bunch didn't really care whether he exed Rainey's name or not. The time was already past when another last vote either way could make any difference. What these weedbenders had in mind was to rag him into starting something, into commencing some overt action they'd been carefully primed to finish. It was a craving in their eyes; it was a feeling pushing at him like the flat of a bony hand.

He managed to smile at them thinly. They wanted something that would give Dink Fraesfield a chance to get his teeth into Muleshoe.

He rested both rope-scarred hands on the horn of his saddle. "If that's so, it's so, I reckon," he replied with assumed indifference.

The man who had snickered shoved away from the building. He wore no hat and showed a narrow bullet-bald head hunched into a pair of thrust-forward shoulders that were cocked for trouble. "Thought mebbe," he sneered, "you'd want to bash someone's face in!"

Left of Mark another bright-eyed walloper put in. "He don't look to be feelin' so cocky as that time he worked Bud Ravenshaw over."

Mark's glance turned a couple of shades darker. But though he was seething inside he managed to keep his mouth buttoned. He fished up his dropped reins and wheeled the roan full around and saw the big beefy face of Ed Journigan before him. "You're getting smart," Journigan grinned, "and if you care for your health you better stay smart. There's a new day about to unfold around Blossom and you cowraisers better be learnin' to walk softly if you don't aim to run afoul of the law."

Mark reined the roan past him and turned out of the yard, hearing the laughs that struck up in his wake. *The poor fools!* he thought. *The poor stinking damned fools!*

The red sun crouched above the mountains like something cut out of cardboard, and the glance he raked over the stockyards held more of worry than a man would ever have gotten him to admit. There'd been wrongs and there was right on both sides of this thing, and each camp was filled with intolerant hotheads who couldn't see in any direction farther than their noses. In the beginning it was the nesters who had fetched in the fences and now the cowmen were using them to keep the farmers out.

There was a middle ground here someplace if the cooler heads would look for it. But what chance did anyone have to solve things peaceable when some skunks in the country were spending all their time prodding festering sores and spreading their corrosive poisons with lies and manufactured "incidents"? Events, Mark thought, were shaping toward a blowoff that would bathe this range in stubborn men's blood.

He'd tried to talk with Eph before about this and had thought he was making some headway until Curly had come back and put his oar into it. Now the Old Man wouldn't even discuss it.

The thing was simple enough boiled down to basic essentials. Some land was good for crops and some wasn't. Give the land that was to the plow-chasers and graze what couldn't be used for farming. This made sense, as Mark had declared, but Curly with lips peeled back had retorted they would be overstocked if they did anything so crazy. And when Mark had suggested they might breed better cattle Eph's son had said bitterly with grim finality he'd be damned if he'd give up one solitary acre of the empire his father had carved from the wilderness and given the best part of his life battling·Indians, droughts and long-loopers to hang onto.

The other big owners, Mark knew, felt the same. But there was going to be trouble. Big trouble. Gun trouble. For months Ed Journigan had been inflaming the hoemen by continual harping on their hardships and miseries; but while bewailing the inequities of their present situation he'd been slyly enticing additional weedbenders into coming here until the tribe now outnumbered the cow crowd three to one.

Muleshoe's range boss shook his head.

It was going to be dark before they got those steers all shut up in their boxcars. Already the sun was half dropped behind the mountains and Mark, having sampled the temper of these hoemen, was strongly inclined to have a talk with his outfit. His final reason for rejecting this impulse sprang from the fear it might in some way accomplish the very thing he sought to avoid.

Cowhands as a group are pretty rugged individualists. Though generally loyal to their salt they tend to have a high regard for old traditions and personal liberty. Any restraint he might place on their freedom of choice and action would be more apt to precipitate trouble than prevent it.

So he took his worries with him, forking his roan up the potholed street toward the unpainted fronts of the town's business houses. Already a few lamps back of unshuttered windows set up oblongs of brightness where the homes of the more affluent thrust their variegated roofs against the slate and cerise of the darkening sky. A chill wind swirled down off the slopes of the Whetstones and the smell of coming winter was strongly in the air.

Mark saw more people on the street and congregated about the fronts of the buildings than he could remember ever having seen before. If it was Journigan's intention to make a show of strength he had sure as hell done it. The place was bulging at the seams. Everywhere he looked there were people in knots or moving. Earth stained men in patched and faded odds and ends smelling of sweat and the plowshare. Arm-waving townsmen. Pot-bellied merchants in shiny white collars below clean scrubbed faces and calculating stares. And there were quite a few women — a heap more than normal — sun-bonneted and laughing or laying the law down through the squalls of their offspring. And all jawing, excitedly or earnestly according to their bent.

He thought the drone of their voices reminiscent of locusts. Where had they all come from? What magic did Free Grass Journigan possess that he'd been able to convince so many this bleak flat around Blossom was the Promised Land?

He swung a glance at the Alhambra but did not turn aside. He saw a handful of men in big hats and spurred boots scornfully watching the crowds from the recess of its porch and several of these called to him. Muleshoe's ramrod lifted a hand but kept the roan's nose aimed at Ching's barber pole.

He was almost abreast of the Lone Star Livery when a team driven by a gaunt straw-hatted farmer, swinging directly in front of him, forced him to pull up. The wagon, rumbling past him, was loaded high with household furnishings, and swinging bare legs from its tailgate lolled a girl, a big girl with a mop of red hair, whose yellow eyes looked back at him boldly.

The livery's runway was blocked by a wagon already waiting there. The nester stopped with the back end of his outfit not over ten feet from the nose of Mark's horse. The girl's full mouth curved in a smile that showed a lot of white teeth, and Mark reached up and dragged off his hat. "Hi," she said. "I'm Lyla. Who are you?"

Muleshoe's ramrod said, "Mark Dawson."

She tried the fit of it on her tongue and smiled again. Mark found it exciting.

She raised one eyebrow and a corner of her mouth. "I guess," she said, "you're what they call a 'cow boy', aren't you?"

"I've sure as heck rode after plenty of cattle." He said: "I'm foreman of Muleshoe."

"Sure — of course. And I'm Queen of the May," she said, laughing. And then, abruptly, she looked up, her eyes searching his queerly. "No kidding?"

"Ask anyone."

"Imagine that!"

He found her interest strangely flattering. She had a nose that was attractively Mongoloid, wide and flaring of nostril, the bridge of it piquantly dusted with freckles. Her eyes, he thought, were as brightly appraising as those of a child; and he found other things, too, which gave weight to this impression of youthfulness on her part. Her dress, too short and plainly made from cheap material, had been carelessly used and was besmirched with dust and rumpled. Her red hair was tousled, loosely braided in the back, and fell over her shoulders in pigtails tied with ribbon. And she was barefoot, too. There was nothing childish, however, about the look of her body.

Her eyes, following his throughout this tour about her person, didn't suggest that she was put out none. "You've got nice muscles, too," she grinned and Mark, feeling suddenly uncommonly warm, said stiffly, nodding his head at her, "I'm powerful proud to have met you, ma'am —"

"Do you have to go now?" She sounded disappointed.

"Reckon maybe I'd better."

"You'll be at the schoolhouse dance tonight, won't you?"

"Matter of fact, I didn't know there was one."

She laughed again, softly. "Us weedbenders is having it to set up Fraesfield's star packin'." She put her arms behind her head, looking up at him provocatively. Her calico dress didn't have any sleeves, just wide ruffles going over the shoulders, and the way she had her arms reared back he could see mighty plain she wasn't wearing no stays.

They looked at each other and Mark's heart got to thumping his chest so hard he reckoned she would have to be deaf not to hear it.

She said, "Reckon you'd be scared to carry me, Muleshoe?"

Still holding his hat he was three doors past the Chinaman's before he woke up. He called himself seven kinds of a fool. But he was in for it now; he had promised to take her.

First hot and then cold, all the time he was waiting his turn at the tub he kept mulling it over, thinking about her and about the damn mess he had let himself in for. He thought, *Cripes, I ought to be bored for the simples!*

He'd probably never live it down. If nothing worse came of it folks' tongues would get to wagging like they was hinged in the middle. Eph Thorpe's ramrod carrying a nester woman to a plow-chaser's hoedown!

And there was Curly to be thought of.

He felt like a man in a shaking fever. What in Tophet would she wear? Would she fix herself up or would she go in them pigtails? Lord! Just the thought of it put goose bumps all over him. He hoped to hell she had some shoes and sense enough to get into them.

By the time he'd stretched himself out in Ching's chair, and been lulled by the sound of Ching stropping his razor, Mark's reflections had worked around to the shape of her again and he didn't feel quite so damned sorry. His disturbance began to be tinged with excitement as he recalled the tight stretch of that cloth across the front of her.

Just the same he'd been a numbskull and he couldn't help being worried, not so much for himself as on account of old Eph. He could imagine what some folks might try to make out of it. Biggest danger though was that he'd get in a fight and that Eph's enemies would seek to use the brawl to touch off the smoldering resentment between the two factions.

Pride wouldn't let him back out of it now though. After all, he told himself, if he were reasonably careful and could remember to keep a tight hold on his temper, there was a fair-to-middling chance he might come out of this dido with no great damage done, except to what some horses' necks might think about his judgment. He reckoned he could stand that. Guessed he'd probably have to.

Curly'd be the worst, all right.

He felt Ching lift off the towels and brush some powder on his face. He got out of the chair and paid his bill and went outside and climbed into the saddle.

He rode over to Syd's Cafe and after he'd got a steak under his belt he was able to look on his forthcoming escapade with a little less censure and a lot more enthusiasm. Hell, a man was entitled to bust over the traces once in a while!

"Lyla," he said, and liked the sound of it better.

He rode across to the hotel and then remembered his horse hadn't fed yet and turned him back up the street through the hoof-tracked dust and into the runway that led to the livery. It lay black in the heavy shadows of the trees but he could see, against the light from the barn lantern, that the wagons had been moved out of it. He wasn't bothered by this, knowing he could find Lyla when he was ready for her. She had said she would meet him along the schoolhouse lane.

He left his roan with the hostler and retraced his way down the still noisy street until checked by a hail from the Alhambra's porch. Crane, the range boss for Terrapin, stepped down and a second, more angular shape quit the group silhouetted against the bright windows and became White Howlett, top screw at Jugwagon. Both men showed grim faces.

"Well, Joe's lost it," Crane said, and Mark nodded soberly. "I'm afraid Muleshoe kind of let old Joe down."

"Wouldn't have made no difference if your whole crowd had voted. Fraesfield got it by a two-thirds majority."

"Offered to keep Joe on as under sheriff," Howlett growled. "I look for trouble with that guy."

Crane nodded darkly. "There'll be trouble, all right, if he tries tearin' down any of Terrapin's fences."

Mark let it ride. "You fellers going to that hoedown?"

Crane peered like a man who had just

24

broke his glasses. "Think I'd shake my hoof with a bunch of damn churn-twisters? I'd sooner be found dead —"

"Maybe you will if you go round talking that way." Mark said flatly, "The sooner we get these chips off our shoulders and make up our minds those birds are halfway human —"

"What the hell you been drinkin'?"

Mark looked at the man and grinned a little grimly. "I'm serious, Howlett. The ranch crowd ain't the only ones that's got rights in this country. Things are —"

Crane put an arm out. "Let me get this straight. Do I understand you're allowin' we ought to start kissin' nesters?"

Several of that bunch on the porch picked their ears up and Mark, self-consciously scowling, said, "What I'm trying to get across is if we don't want this range to become another Wind River we better start mixing a little Christian charity —"

"This Thorpe's idea you're pushin'?" asked Howlett, and a kind of grim quiet shut out the street's noises.

Mark saw three or four of that bunch crane their necks and he got suddenly warm as he considered how this would look when they learned about him taking that girl to the·schoolhouse.

25

"No," he said tightly. "As range boss of Muleshoe I back the same view as the rest of you, but —"

"You can't have it both ways," Crane said coldly. "The man we intrust with our defense against squatters —"

"They're not squatters," Mark growled.

Howlett tapped Mark's chest. "You can't run with the hares an' hunt with the hounds. Get off the fence, Dawson."

"I'm not on any fence. I back Eph Thorpe's play regardless. But that don't hide from me the truth of this business." Mark's voice, edged with anger, went up three swift notches. "These nesters are getting a raw deal and you know it!"

Every eye on that porch slapped shocked and hard against his features. He could feel the shrinking back of these men's minds from contact with him. He had branded himself a pariah.

Howlett looked at him and spat. "I'll have no mealy-mouthed bastard tel—"

Mark hit him so quick and so hard along the jaw the burly Jugwagon boss was flung almost around before, caught in his spurs, he crashed into the porch rail. He hung there a moment, spreadeagled against it, then he pulled himself up and slammed a hand at his holster.

"Watch yourself, White! He's not armed," Crane's voice grumbled.

Raging, furious, Howlett snarled. "Then let him *get* armed! No bunch-quittin' nester-lovin' son of a —"

"That's enough, White. Just drop it," a tall black-stetsoned man said, coming forward. "We got enough troubles shaping without scrapping among ourselves. Go round up your men and get them headed for the ranch."

In the frozen glow of his outraged passions the Jugwagon boss appeared minded to go on with it but finally let his hand drop and went tramping off to do as he'd been ordered. Pell, the Jugwagon owner, swept a bleak glance over Mark and, turning on his heel, pushed through the crowd of wooden-cheeked cowhands and passed through the swinging doors of the Alhambra.

Crane sighed and said, "A house divided . . ." and let the rest go with a weary shrug. Mark, still scowling, moved away from the saloon, still feeling the hostile stares of the porch crowd; striding down the warped planks he went into the hotel.

The clerk, seated back of his counter, was very much engrossed in braiding a hair rope. Mark didn't bother him. He took a look at the book and went up the creaking stairs and along the balcony. When he found the right number he put his fist to the door. He caught the groan of bed springs, the rattle of paper. Bare feet approached and a man's voice called through further crackling, "Who is it?"

"Muleshoe ramrod."

"What do *you* want?"

"Check for that herd."

After a moment of silence Mark heard the rasp of a key being turned. The door opened and through a reek of cheap cigar smoke he saw a bald-headed man in glasses with his teeth out attempting to hide his red flannels behind a three-days-old copy of the Brewery Gulch *Gazette*.

Mark had difficulty reconciling this querulous apparition with the derby-hatted buyer who'd stood across from Lefty Red keeping tally at the stockyards. It was the same man, however, and he said as though fed up with the business, "How many times you want to be paid for them cattle?"

"I haven't *been* paid yet —"

"You can read, I guess, can't you?"

Forgetful of his bizarre appearance the man, letting go of his newsprint, padded over to the chair where his clothes were draped out and came back with a paper which he thrust irritably at Mark. "Anything wrong with that?"

"I guess not," Mark said. It was a perfectly good bill of sale signed by Curly. "I didn't know Mr. Thorpe was taking care of the payoff."

The buyer said bitterly, "I didn't, either. Nor I didn't expect to have to ride clean to Bisbee to provide it in cash."

Mark said, dumbfounded, "In *cash?*"

"That's right. Thorpe got me out of bed at seven-ten this morning to say it had to be in cash or the whole deal was off."

2

Had anyone with malice aforethought been awaiting his reappearance, Mark might easily have been shot quitting the hotel because no part of his mind was on what he was doing. Coming through the light-filled doorway connecting porch with lobby he moved into the street with about as much concern for his surroundings as a sleepwalker.

Why had Curly taken it on himself to collect for this trainload of cattle? To be sure, on his return, the Old Man had made Curly manager; but so far as Mark knew the ranch had done well this year and it wasn't like Eph to switch plans and say nothing. His last words to Mark before they'd all left to get at this fall roundup had been to bank the check he would get for the beef. It was quite all right for Curly to step into this, either as manager or as son of the owner, but Mark was minded to know why he had done so, and why he had insisted on being paid in currency. In a town considered a "bad place to have your gun stick" Mark thought Eph's son was being unduly brash.

Most of the cow crowd had gone other places by the time he got back to the Alhambra. After a brief look around he pushed through the swinging doors.

Like most shipping points in the West of that time more than half the business establishments of Blossom were some kind of deadfalls. Quayle's place was much the largest, a honky-tonk combining liquor with cards and women. Unofficial town hangout for most of the local ranch crews, its custom at the moment was almost solidly composed of men who had no reason to look on cowmen with anything save distrust.

Mark, paused just inside the batwings, let his glance play over the crowd in the hope of picking up Curly. The games, through the blend of smoke and liquor fumes curling like some swamp miasma below the lamps' tin reflectors, did not appear to be particularly prosperous but the bar, to Mark's surprise, was packed three deep. Some of his astonishment slacked off a little when he caught sight of Journigan at the mahogany's far end with a comradely arm thrown about Fraesfield's shoulder. The former cowman-turned-landshark was probably setting them up in celebration of the fellow's election victory.

They looked to be in fine spirits and Mark, not seeing Curly and having little desire to be crowed at by Journigan, moved off through the crowd toward the bar's other end. He had his glance on the prowl, still hoping to see Curly, when he inadvertently bumped into a man. "Watch where you're going," a voice growled in his ear. Mark, not wanting any trouble, murmured a gruff apology and, turning, found himself looking into the bleak eyes and expressionless features of a man known locally as Dog Town Slim, a tough character who had lately blown in with the dust from the Tombstone stage. Considering the fellow's unwinking glance Mark wondered if Howlett had given the man a job.

He stepped around the gunman gingerly, not knowing what to expect but ready to do some mighty fast moving should the fellow give the appearance of intending to carry this further. The man's hard stare stayed unreadably on him for another long moment, then Mark was past.

He moved along down the room with muscles taut, his roving glance still attempting to locate Curly. It seemed pretty plain the Muleshoe manager had gone elsewhere. Mark fervently hoped he was on his way home. For Eph's sake.

He told himself he was being childish to resent Curly's interference. But he still couldn't like it. Perhaps it was the way Curly'd gone about the business, riding off before daylight with never a word about his real intentions, letting Mark imagine it was a letter he was rushing to town for when all the time his only reason for hurry had been to make sure he'd get the payoff in cash. There was something —

He saw Quayle and veered toward him. "Curly Thorpe been around?"

The Alhambra's owner was a gross, paunch-bellied man, florid and bland with a paraded bonhomie as false as the smile of Judas. Splinters of light danced from the puffy-fingered paw he raised in jovial greeting, and he rolled a fat cigar between his thick and moist red lips as his cold eyes studied Mark shrewdly. "Spent the bulk of the day here playin' cards with Jack Teen and some cowmen from Texas."

Teen was one of Quayle's housemen, a real high-roller who had learned his craft in the dives of Juarez. Mark said in tight-lipped irony, "Curly clean 'em out, did he?"

Quayle showed a gold-toothed grin.

33

"When you goin' to let that boy grow up, Dawson?"

"What'd you do with his shirt?"

"Oh, it wasn't that bad. He didn't drop much this trip."

"Where's he at now?"

Quayle took the cigar from his mouth and considered it. "I expect your guess would be as good as mine." He brought his glance back up and sent a look about the room. "He quit my place about three hours ago."

"Alone?"

"I think he went off with that cowman. If you want to wait here a minute —"

"Not that important. If he happens to come back just tell him I been looking for him."

Outside Mark, chancing to swing a backward look into the place across the batwings, saw Dog Town Slim drifting toward the back room. Ed Journigan, moving in the same direction, was about ten steps ahead of him.

Mark sighed and shook his head. "Never rains but it pours." He watched the pair a moment; then, wheeling, quit the porch. On a hunch he went a couple doors down, cut north up an alley and cautiously prowled the trash until the back of the Alhambra loomed blackly before him. As he came nearer he discerned the dim shapes of cobwebbed dusty windows. There was light behind them but the shades were drawn. He could hear a dim murmur of voices and, with the thought that Curly's might be one of them, he warily tried a sash but it was either locked or stuck. He tried the other window then with no better result.

He stood a moment in thought. It was possible Quayle had Curly behind those windows but it was much more likely, if Muleshoe's manager were in the place at all, that he would be sampling the entertainment afforded upstairs. Mark couldn't go busting up there looking for him without inviting some pretty robust reactions.

He went back to the street. Knowing Curly as he did from having practically grown up with him he would have bet quite a stack of chips Eph's son was someplace playing cards or had got hold of a woman. Curly, Mark remembered, considered himself quite a connoisseur.

He set off up the street, deciding to make the rounds. It wasn't so much Curly that was on Mark's mind as it was the idea of Curly tomcatting around with all that Muleshoe cash in his pockets.

It took him about an hour to comb the rest of the saloons and the town's parlor houses. He didn't find Curly in any of them. By the time he'd got done Mark had reached the far west edge of Blossom and was down by the stockyards along the railroad sidings in a region dingily cluttered with the tents and tarpaper shanties thrown up by an influx of nesters Journigan's activities hadn't managed to locate yet. The schoolhouse, set back in its pasture, was a quarter of a mile off to the south of him and the guitar and fiddle sounds coming from it suddenly reminded him of Lyla.

He was of two minds about her by this time. The practical workaday side of his nature assured him he'd be smart to forget all about her. Why lay himself open to all the things any dalliance with her was inviting? Common sense assured him they had nothing in common and the ordered run of his thoughts vociferously insisted there could be no place for a nester's woman in the life of Muleshoe's range boss.

But common sense wasn't everything, Mark's youth assured him. He wanted another taste of that strange unreal world her exciting personality had so briefly opened to him. He kept remembering her red hair and the way she had looked at him with the cloth of her dress so tautly stretched across the front of her. She hadn't looked like the kind who would wait around long — or have to.

It was this last thought which decided him. He said, "To hell with hunting Curly." The guy was old enough to look out for himself and no one had constituted Mark Curly's keeper. Certainly Curly wouldn't thank him!

He struck off across lots for the shine of the schoolhouse lamps.

A little later there'd be a moon but right now the stars looked down on him like brilliants scattered across black velvet. The wind had dropped and the night was brisk with a lot of good smells to it. Mark found his pulses racing with the prospect of holding that girl in his arms. He hadn't gone to many dances but he reckoned he could get through *Sally Gooden* and probably one or two others, simple things like *Texas Star.* He could picture those golden eyes laughing up at him and reckoned hard work could be overdone a little.

He was picking his way through a bunch of thrown-out cans and discarded whiskey bottles when he rounded the back side of a shack and came into a dusty wagon-rutted road. Other shacks, on the far side, foreshortened his view and, not being able at the moment to see the schoolhouse, he stopped, trying to orient himself by the music.

Some of these shacks had lights behind their curtains and he briefly tried to visualize what sort of life went on inside them. The fiddles and guitars seemed to be taking time out and, during this silent interlude, he heard the nearby squall of a yelling child and a man's harsh voice telling the kid to shut up. Then renewed fiddle sound wailed into the night as the bunch at the schoolhouse swung into a reel. Mark, turning left, moved off up the road.

He had not gone very far and was deep in the shadow of overhanging cottonwoods when a man up ahead loomed vaguely into view, cutting diagonally across the thick dust of the road and losing himself, rather abruptly, between shacks.

Although he had not caught any very good look at him something about the fellow's gait gnawed its way through Mark's memory and he stared after the man, frowning. It was incredible to imagine he'd been looking at Curly — absolutely fantastic. Nothing could have lured a dude of Curly's elegant notions into prowling the dark poralee of any region as squalid as this.

Mark pulled his glance from the shadows and tramped on, snorting softly, rather indignantly, at the way Curly'd taken hold of his mind these last few weeks. Curly'd probably gone home soon after quitting the Alhambra.

Mark came into the lane tugging down the brim of his hat against the light blazing out of the schoolhouse and had a quick look around for Lyla. Not seeing the girl, he moved on toward the box elder thicket, wondering if she had given him up. He couldn't blame her if she had after the way he had kept her standing around. He moved into the trees, still hoping, but didn't see her.

He stood there a few minutes, moodily listening to the music. Then he quit the shadows, strolling over to the bunch of slicked-up grangers standing around outside the door. They didn't notice him at first. Most of those on the porch were watching the dancers. Some of the others were still hashing over the results of the election and several of the younger bucks, heads bent, were swapping coarse jokes if one were to judge by the guffaws. A lanky man in this group, slapping his thigh, partly turned in his laughter and abruptly went still as something hacked out of stone. All the lecherous mirth dropped away from his cheeks and his protuberant stare became as glassily fixed as a shotgunned rabbit's.

Other heads began to turn. Talk fell into a tightening silence through which the wail of the fiddles came with wild abandon. A burly fellow to the left of Mark found voice to say: "Kinda off your range, ain'tcha?"

"It's a free country —"

"Is it?" The man considered Mark's boots, rubbed a glance across Mark's high-crowned hat. "Lot of my neighbors ain't found it that way. Wherever they've turned they've come up ag'in' fences."

Mark looked around. "I don't see no fence here."

He stepped onto the porch, hearing the low growls rumbling back of their teeth, aware of their hate and ignoring it. He sent his glance through a window, watching the gyrating sets of the dancers whirl against the stacked desks and the soured resignation on the faces of wall flowers.

The saw of bows and strumming fingers presently ceased their mesmeric movements, cramped backs straightened and the violinists took their fiddles from chins as the clapping crowd commenced to leave the floor, laughing and chatting, color high, faces shining. Mark's eyes found Lyla on the arm of a slat-shaped spare faced man in clean but faded and threadbare denim. Mark stared closely at this one, and then he

40

pushed through the door, unmindful of hard glances, intercepting the pair as the man was about to steer the girl to a bench.

Mark, carefully keeping his eyes off the girl, asked, "How you making it, Rube?"

"Why, you danged ol' hoss, you! Where the hell you been hibernatin'?" He reached forward, grinning, grabbing and pumping Mark's hand. "Ain't seen your mug since the time Jim Wolf ran that tramp outa Charleston! You still workin' for Eph?"

Mark nodded, sobering. Once he and this man had been saddle pards holding down the same Muleshoe linecamp. But that had been before Rube got the itch to own land and choused off into the Cherrycows to start a haywire outfit. The venture hadn't lasted on account of longloopers. When the government had thrown the country open to homesteading, and before the big ranchers had started fencing folks out, he'd come down onto the flats to try his hand at dry-farming. Mark reckoned he was still at it for Rube Krieger was stubborn. "Whyn't you quit cockleburrin' around?" Mark said, and Krieger grinned.

"Whyn't you come help me? Give me time an' a little water an' I'll make a crop yet! I've got alfalfa up to my kneecap; alls I need is a little rain. One good wettin' will do it."

41

"Don't you know," Mark said, "the oldest frogs in this country haven't ever got wet?"

Krieger's craggy face broke into a chuckle. "Hell, it's not *that* bad." He took hold of Mark's arm. "Here, I want you to meet the most girl for her size that's ever come west of the Mizery river — Lyla St. Clair. Lyla, this here's the ranny they call Mister Muleshoe, the work-dodgin' soft-soapin' cow-proddin' galoot who, through no merit of his own unless it's keepin' his mouth shut, has riz from the ranks to be Eph Thorpe's top screw. If you can't pronounce Muleshoe he'll answer to Mark Dawson."

Dragging off his hat Mark twisted his head. She'd got fixed up, all right. Her red hair, arranged now in neck puffs coiled and soft as the gut of a squirrel, gleamed like pennies just out of the mint. She was fresh and sweet as a clean sprig of sage against the sweat smell stuffing this overpacked room. She'd wrapped herself into some kind of olive-colored thing that slimmed down her waist and made her breasts stand out like the muscles on a blacksmith. Mark felt the heat creeping up around his collar. He thought she might just as well have come dressed in a banana skin.

Rube was explaining she was new to this

country but, after seeing that getup, no one had to tell Mark. She was giving no mind to the stares focused on her. She was looking straight back at him, frank as a man; and just as soberly she said, "Hi, Muleshoe. Guess you'll be cravin' to jerk my arm?"

"Well, if Rube's got no objections —"

"There's the music, lunkhead. Fly at it," Rube said, shoving him toward her.

Mark never did find out what they were supposed to be doing. The caller, clapping his hands, yowled out:

"Hang the dogs an' kill the cats —
Double yo' dose of rough on rats.
Swing the cow an' now the calf,
Now yo' partner once an' a half."

Sometimes she was briefly in front of him, gravely probing with her golden stare; other times she was to his left or to his right or completely lost someplace behind. Hands jerked his arms and hauled him around while the whole world dizzily spun in a circle. Now they were romping across the floor, two by two, with elbows hooked. The men howled like Comanches, the ladies squealed. Another girl whirled him and chased him back. Lyla, locking her feet to the floor, grabbed his wrists and swung him around.

43

"Big fun, ain't it?"

"Tell you better," Mark gasped, "after I've caught up with myself!"

She didn't laugh or giggle the way a lot of girls would, just kept delving into him with that translucent stare, the feel of her fingers, strong and cool, guiding him through the frenzied gyrations. The old guffer setting the pace leaped onto a desk top, stamping and clapping.

"Haul off yo' shoes an' smell yo' socks,
Grab you a heifer an' rattle yo' hocks.
A little mo' sass an' a little mo' gravy —
Once an' a half an' swing yo' baby!"

The room barreled into another whirl and when Mark came out of it Lyla was gone and he was snagged to the bulges of a billowy matron who, smothering him into her ample front, sashayed him down the stomping lane. Other hands caught him and spun him around and a tall skirted beanpole with pipe-stem arms lugged him back to his place at a gallop. Lyla said, "You're doin' real well."

Mark had no chance to see if she were laughing. The third girl whisked him away in a whirl. He saw Lyla pass and then she had hold of him. "You known Rube long?"

44

he managed to pant. "About half an hour," she called over her shoulder; then the cornfed filly twisted his arm and, when vision returned, there was Lyla directly before him, watching him gravely with that pulse-thumping stare.

"Hands in yo' pockets an' neck to the
      wall,
Take a chaw of tobaccer an' promenade
      all."

Mark sleeved sweat. "How much longer's this keep up?"

"That's all," Lyla said, catching hold of his hands. The guitars thumped out a throbbing bar and the fiddles sawed into a reverberant silence. Talk started up and Lyla steered him into a bunch of still clapping, still flushed bench-headed couples that were beginning to break clear of the milling confusion. "Not tired, are you?"

"Gosh, no!" Mark lied.

"I am," she said, and leaned against him a little. "Let's get outside a spell. Expect I'm needin' a breath of fresh air."

Mark reckoned he could pretty well do with one himself and was turning her toward the door to the porch when she tugged at his arm. "Not that way, Muleshoe. You wantin' to be stared at by all them boys?"

For a fact Mark wasn't too sold on the notion. He followed her toward the punch stand at the rear. He got her a cupful and had one himself; and while they stood drinking he saw the gaunt farmer who'd been driving her wagon. The guy was perched on the sill of an across-the-room window jawing with the fellow Mark had exchanged words with earlier, the bib-overalled one who had given it as his opinion Joe Rainey would be lucky if he didn't get run out of town. They were both watching Mark and their expressions were not pleasant.

Lyla nudged Mark and swung her glance to the left. Mark, looking that way, saw a door in the corner beyond the stacked-up desks. He looked again toward the pair in the window but some of the bunch about the punch stand cut off his view. Shrugging, he set down his emptied cup and with a mounting excitement went through the door after her.

"Reckon you'd care to set awhile under them trees off yonder?"

The night was filled with restless shadows but the moon was up and by its silvery light he was able to make out the place she had in mind. This was half across the meadow making a solid blotch of darkness south of the stream meandering through it. Mark, staring a moment, abruptly nodded. "Suits me."

"Then I better take off these stockin's," she said. "I don't see no sense gettin' them snagged in the weeds."

She sat down on the stoop and got out of her shoes. "How you like these glad rags?" she asked, peering up at him.

"Some flashy," Mark managed, not mentioning he'd seen girls at Quayle's that looked a lot more covered up.

She said, "Boughten stuff just don't hang on me right. Made this one myself." He caught a flash of white leg as she pulled off a stocking. "I'm pretty handy at makin' things fit. Don't go much for buttons — too apt to get tore off. Hooks're handier and show a sight less wrinkles."

She wriggled her toes and got up, putting a hand on his arm as she bent to tug on one of those high button shoes. She had quite a time with it and Mark, with the moon playing over the low dip of her neckline, became extremely engrossed in the beauties of nature. He suddenly realized she was watching him. With her face tipped in shadow he couldn't make out her expression. She came upright without hurry and smoothed her dress at the hips. "Reckon I won't bother to button them."

They considered each other for a couple of moments.

"Sure a pretty night, ain't it?"

"Never seen a prettier."

Neither of them thought to look at it. "Here —" she made a ball of her stockings, "put these in your pocket. You ain't got any steeples in it, have you?"

"Steeples . . . ?"

"Them little U-shape things you-uns put up your bob wire with."

Mark, chuckling, shook his head. She grinned a little, too, like it was something shared between them. She said after a moment, "You still aimin' to go?"

He took her arm and they set out.

They could see the pale twinkle of the creek off ahead and, over to the left, the scattered lights of the town; they weren't thinking much about these though. The air had a tingling, strange exciting kind of dampness and the night was pungent with the smell of growing green things.

Mark reckoned he was being considerable of a fool but not even for a moment was he notioned to call it off. The pleasant fragrance of her nearness awakened hungers too long neglected and he was suddenly impatient to reach the obscurity of the trees.

They reached the creek and he carried her over it, wondering what she would do if he slipped off the rocks and doused both of them. He didn't slip but, after they'd got across, he stood a moment looking back over the meadow before, setting her down, he followed her into the pooled gloom of the cottonwoods.

It was not so black in here as he'd imagined and, now that they were here, he felt uncertain, edgily nervous lest he'd read more into this deal than intended.

They stood silent for several heartbeats, unwinkingly watching each other, not moving. Then he reached out and pulled her to him, minded to know how far she would go with this. Locked in his arms she made no outcry, no resistance. Under that olive-colored thing she had on he could feel the tumultuous pounding of her heart. Her thighs came against his. His lips found her mouth and time lost all meaning.

She was panting, trembling, when he let her go. She put her hands to her hair, brought it tumbling about her shoulders and stood, heavily breathing, watching him, waiting, saying never a word but moving readily with him when he turned deeper into the grove's loamy shadows. Not until the far gleam of the schoolhouse lamps was shut away by the intervening trunks did he wheel, again to pull her roughly against him.

But she shook her head. Catching hold of his hands she drew him into a still more impenetrable blackness, there melting against him; and when his head came down to find the sweetness of her mouth the tips of her fingers dug into his shoulders.

The want in Mark was terrible as fever but a piece of his mind was still rebelliously busy. Not thinking of this but of the later, other things this could lead to, of the smoldering bitterness that was dividing this country, that was turning old friends into snarling dogs.

"What is it?" Lyla whispered; and the wild fragrance of her hair, of her warm breath and supple body made tatters of his caution, raising desires he could not block. She'd led him here and she was willing and he closed his arms around her, then turned cold and rigid with listening.

There was someone else in this grove, someone close, someone stealthily edging nearer on the balls of invisible feet.

Mark's arms fell away from her. The shadows stirred like smoke and the miniature explosion of a snapped twig rushed into the vacuum of the girl's caught breath. The rasp of a match scratched through the ugly quiet. And above that guttering flame, near almost enough that he could have reached out and struck them, two leering faces took shape.

To Mark this whole episode was suddenly cheap and degrading. Disgust curled his lips and a sick shame for his stupidity filled his throat with a taste of nausea. Cold rage churned through him then but he knew better than to move with the shine of metal glinting in Dink Fraesfield's lifted fist.

3

Rube Krieger in his thorough German way had looked a long while to find a woman he could settle down with and had come near deciding he had found her when the red-haired Lyla had shown up in town two weeks ago. She was big-boned enough to be some help around the place. Didn't wear a man out with a lot of fool talk. He'd discovered she could cook. In fact she'd only one real drawback and this, being her looks, he considered sufficiently serious that he was still of two minds about her.

He wasn't bothered about her past. What he wanted was a good rugged woman with enough fire in her to keep his bed and her own damn feet warm. He reckoned she had the fire, all right. But he sure wasn't craving no woman he'd be all the time getting into trouble over.

Too good looking and a heap too friendly. He shook his head morosely as he watched

Mark follow her out the back door. He didn't blame Mark for following her. Half the men in this town had their eyes on Lyla and Rube didn't think marriage would discourage them any.

He went out on the porch and strode around to the side and, moving through the old gaffers and callow youths swapping jokes around the barrel, helped himself to a drink. Putting down the tin dipper he circled back to the front again and saw Mark, mouth tight and eyes filled with cold anger, coming into the lane closely followed by Fraesfield and Journigan.

Rube turned clear around to stare after them, now catching the dark shine of something in Fraesfield's fist. Eyes scrinched and gone narrow he watched these three head toward Blossom's main drag.

"By Judas," he muttered. "What hell's broth's cookin' now?"

He'd never had much use for Fraesfield, privately considering him little better than a boot licker. And now he thought about this and about the way Mark had quit the dance to go clomping out after Lyla; and he reckoned it was plenty queer, Mark going off now with that pair.

He sauntered casually after them, tagging along far enough in their wake to make cer-

tain they were bound for jail like he'd figured; after which he turned back and
combed the schoolyard for Lyla, whom he
wasn't able to locate. He hunched his shoulders against a tree then and tried to figure
out what kind of deal had come off here.

He recalled seeing the gaunt nester who'd
driven Lyla's wagon into this country sitting
on a window sill in converse with Gunter, a
man he'd never cottoned to from the moment
he'd first come across him. The bib-overalled
Gunter had a quarter section down along Ten
Mile Creek, some of the best bottom land in
the country, which no plow had ever broken.
Lot of the homesteader crowd reckoned he
must have come with money but Rube
nursed different notions having twice observed the man in very queer places holding
talk with Free Grass Journigan.

Rube had his own notions about Journigan, too, and putting all these thoughts together reckoned it was time he was moving
yonderly. Swinging off across lots in the
cowman's boots he had never forsaken he
came presently in sight of the shack used by
Lyla while she waited for Journigan to find
her some land.

He observed that a lamp was lit behind
pulled curtains. He was of the rather jaun-
diced opinion that if she'd had company the

lamp would be out. By nature cautious, however, he approached the place quietly and so was still in the dooryard when he caught the growl of voices.

He melted back into the shadow of scrub oaks and hunkered down to await developments. Two men in there by the sound of what he'd heard and, while he couldn't be sure, he would have given odds Journigan was one of them.

He was correct. In about five minutes light spilled away from the opening door and broody as he was Rube noticed no screak of hinges. He saw a man step into the dust of the yard while a second, larger shape, broadly pausing in the lamp glow, angrily snarled, "You better learn to use your favors where they'll do you a little good."

The girl said something Rube wasn't quite able to catch. Then Journigan rasped with a frustrated fury: "You'll git no land around here, let me tell you, till you climb down off that high hoss an' do somethin' to earn it! Alls I'm askin —"

"I heard you the first time."

"Don't figure because you're a woman you're goin' to get anywhere buckin' me. I'm big taters in this man's country, an'll be a heap bigger. I don't aim to let no man stand in my shadder — nor any flibberty-gip hank of calico, neither! Keep outa my way if you don't want to git hurt."

"You threatenin' to kill me?"

"Killin's fer fools! I got ways of dealin' with stubbornness. They ain't pretty an' you won't like 'em. Just remember that, missy, next time I come by here."

He strode off without bothering to close the door, Fraesfield's shape swinging into step behind him. The girl remained in the lamplight staring after them a moment before she turned and pushed the door shut.

Rube stayed where he was silently squatted in the shadows another ten minutes to give them time to get gone. Then he got to his feet and slipped around the far side and quietly thumped on a window.

"Who's there?"

"Rube. Douse that light an' unlatch the back entry."

Darkness blacked out the window. "Never guessed you was bashful," she said, letting him in.

"I got a proper regard for local politics," Rube grunted. "What'd that precious pair want?"

"They've got that Muleshoe ridin' boss locked in the calaboose. I were minded to get a little closer acquainted and taken him into them schoolhouse cottonwoods. They throwed a pistol gun on him. They come here to get me to X a writin' makin' out he —"

Rube growled in the darkness.

"I told them he never done nothin' of the kind. And it were God's own truth," she added, fetching a sigh. Then she said on a brighter note, "But they can't do no hurt to him without my X can they?"

"Not a chance," Rube assured, with more confidence than was warranted. "Keep this place dark an' make sure you got both doors barred. I'm goin' back up town to see what word's around."

He was starting to leave when a sudden frown turned him back to her. "Here — you keep this hogleg handy. You hear anyone nosin' around outside you chuck a bullet at him. I never seen a skunk yet was extry partial to that music."

Trouble was, Rube reflected as he set off through the trash, there were other ways an enterprising jigger like Journigan could get at Mark if he wanted to bad enough. If he'd spread talk around and made it ugly enough, a little free rotgut distributed with some more talk could work up a mob that wouldn't ask to see X's. Some ways, Rube thought, these sodbusters were like sheep.

When he came up to the Alhambra it was about like he'd figured. Peering in over the batwings he couldn't see the bar for the bunch that was packed around it. He could hear the rumble of Journigan's voice.

He didn't wait to catch its message but, ducking across the hoof-tracked dust to the porch of the Aces Up, took a look through one of its dingy windows and saw much the same thing going on. Only here it was Gunter who was slinging the chin sound. And there were too many knots of muttering men on the street.

Rube didn't like it. He had watched trouble building here for too long a time not to recognize the ear marks. A former cowpuncher, he was able to see both sides of what the Homestead Act was bringing on. No cowman wanted to give up range he'd been using all his life to any bunch of fool hoemen bent on plowing his grass up. But the law had been passed. The government wanted this country settled up and every land-hungry farmer had been promised a quarter section that would pull up and move out here. A lot of folks had sold off everything they owned, and a lot who'd never had anything had come out here to get it. If there was a nigger in this woodpile he went, Rube thought, by the name of Ed

Journigan. Feller had no business taking fees to locate people on land the government told them was being given free — particular when he knew damn well the cowmen never aimed to let them have it.

Due to Mark more than likely, who'd been chose to deal with these grangers, there hadn't up to now been any real serious trouble. Journigan had located all he could around these flats. But this ground was all used up now and there were a heap more nesters on hand than was settled. They were beginning to get ugly. Time was a-wasting and they wanted to break ground. Journigan had been promising them a new deal once they got Rainey out of the sheriff's office. It was plain to Rube it was Journigan's plan to use Fraesfield's star when he moved into the hills to call the cow crowd's bluff. If Free Grass had been honest in his guise of helping farmers he'd have called in the government when the ranchers started fencing.

Rube never had reckoned Ed Journigan for honest. What he'd heard at Lyla's only confirmed his dark suspicions. He'd a notion to call in the government himself except he didn't know how to go about it. Wasn't time now anyway. Journigan was just about set to ram these nesters down the cowman's teeth. This dirty move against Mark was meant to split things wide open.

Rube, swearing under his breath, drifted into an alley and set out to cut around to the back of Blossom's jail. Mark was too old a friend and too good a man, by Judas, to get whipsawed around in any rotten deal like this. There wasn't anything else for it but to get him out of that jail. With Journigan's wild talk stoking up their passions and Journigan's whisky rumbling through their bowels, if the farm crowd took Mark away from Fraesfield now he'd be fitted with a choke strap before you could say Jack Robinson.

Rube paused a few seconds to kind of size up his surroundings and, in that interval, caught the plain sound of bootsteps less than ten yards ahead of him. He couldn't see a thing in this thick gloom behind buildings, but now he caught a low mumble of voices and judged by the sounds there were two fellows up there heading for the back of the jail same as he was.

They must have stopped there in the blackness because the next thing he knew he was damn near on top of them. Rube, stiffening, heard one of them say, "That's what he's fixin' to do — jest watch an' you'll see. He didn't hev me put that horse out here for nothin'! I tell you he's got cold feet — he's gonna turn that sonofabuck loose!"

Rube saw the horse then, ground tied by the jail's back door in deep shadow. Only a suggestion of the animal's shape was visible, a portion of neck and shoulder with the solider black of a rifle's butt starkly etched against the moon-dappled flank of Stein's Mercantile.

"Aw, Dink wouldn't do that; he wouldn't dast cross Ed up. You must of misread the —"

"Misread hell! That's the bronc Dawson come in on. You keep your eyes peeled. I'm goin' to fetch some of the boys."

Rube heard him move off, heard the diminishing footfalls fade away around a corner, and bitterly wished he hadn't left his sixgun with Lyla. Very cautiously then he slipped off his boots.

With one of them dangling by its straps from each hand he commenced a stealthy advance. He felt reasonably confident the man was watching the horse but this was damn tricky business. You couldn't ever say what a horse would take it into his mind to do and if one of Rube's feet rammed into a tin can or discarded bottle and set it rolling there would be hell to pay in mighty short order. And, besides all this, he couldn't see the fellow but had to stalk him by guess-work.

He moved deeper into the heavier gloom beside the jail wall. He could see the man now, a blocky looking jasper with a farmer's straw hat on. Rube worked another four steps nearer and saw the horse turn its head, looking around at him, ears pricked forward. Sweat came out on Rube's neck and on the palms of his hands; and the man in front of him grumbled, "What's the matter, boy?"

Rube drew back his right arm.

The roan, snorting, looked ready to spook. The man, suddenly frightened, pulled his shoulders around but he wasn't quite fast enough. The spurless heel of Rube's boot caught him back of an ear and he went down without sound, all his joints limp as doll rags.

Rube quieted the horse.

Pulling on his boots he got the man over a shoulder. He carried him far enough back into the shadows to alleviate the danger of immediate discovery. Using the fellow's belt he lashed the man's wrists and ankles. There was a gun in the pocket where the man kept his handkerchief. Rube took the gun and tied the rag around his mouth. He was straightening from this when he heard the jail's back door open.

No light seeped out and it was closed almost at once. There came a tinkle of spur chains, the creak of stretched leather. Hoof sounds moved away. But Rube's grin washed out when he remembered the fellow who'd gone off to get help.

He hurried around to the front of Stein's Mercantile. The place was still open but Stein's clerk was blowing the lamps out; Stein was helping the last customer get together his purchases. The customer's horse stood sleepily dozing at Stein's hitch rail. Rube unknotted the reins and led the animal around to the back door of the jail.

The ruse might stall pursuit awhile. But not long enough to help Mark much once that other fellow found his watchdog missing. Rube was casting around in his mind for something better when he heard men moving up the alley from the street. Nothing he'd done could help Mark without these fellows were pulled away from here pronto.

He leaped into the saddle of the horse he'd just borrowed, brought the reins whistling down across the animal's rump and took off around the far side of the Mercantile.

Shouts and angry oaths boiled out of the darkness behind him. Rube's lips pulled away from his teeth in a grin. It was working, by Judas — they thought he was Dawson! Now if they'd just think so long enough to come tearing after him there was a pretty fair chance Mark would get clean away.

He whirled the horse left at the front of Stein's store, seeing muzzle lights bloom as he swept past the alley. He raised his captured gun and banged three shots above their heads just to egg them on and, cutting left again around the street's last black building, struck out for the border at a high and wild gallop.

4

Though he spent the balance of that night in the saddle, it was crowding noon of the following day before Mark sighted the first of Muleshoe's wire.

Fraesfield had jugged him for molesting a woman. Like a caught fence-crawler he'd been chucked in the bullpen and Journigan, who had been with Fraesfield when the sheriff had jumped him, had said flat out he would be almighty lucky if he didn't jerk hemp.

After the first long hour of being alone behind bars Mark had begun to think Journigan might turn out to have the right of it. Just prior to Mark's arrest there'd been a chair-throwing brawl between some of Muleshoe's crew and a bunch of riled nesters and feeling, to judge from sounds in the street, had been running pretty high by the time they'd got around to locking Mark up. Two weedbenders had been dangerously mauled and one of the honkytonks just about wrecked before the Muleshoe boys had cut string and departed.

It was the "departed" part of this information which had most heavily weighed on Mark's reflections. Aside from being an unmitigated chump it was plain he had Journigan to thank for this jailing. Big Ed, knowing only that Mark — by Eph's influence — was the man who'd been chosen to rod the discouragement of homesteaders (never suspecting it was due entirely to Mark that no blood had yet been spilled), had cooked up this deal to get him out of the way.

Journigan needed an example, a carefully tailored show of strength, to put new hope into the fools he had lured here. He didn't want them pulling out to spread the truth of real conditions. The election had given him a sheriff and a judge and Mark's presence at that dance — if he had not indeed inspired it — must have seemed the best luck in a month of Sundays. Certainly he had seized opportunity by the forelock and now, with Mark jugged, he was in a position to furnish quite a spectacle. Weedbender bitterness, flaring anew with that saloon brawl and the unrequiting mauling of a pair of beat-up homesteaders, would be in a mood to relish raw meat — so why not toss them Eph Thorpe's range boss? A little more free whisky and a tale of Mark caught in that dark grove with one of their women (and not another Muleshoe hand now in town) ought to be just what the doctor ordered.

Having doped things thus Mark had been more than a little astonished to have Fraesfield come back and release him before events steamed to the inevitable crisis. "What's the matter?" he asked. "Couldn't Doc find enough evidence?"

Fraesfield, who had always reminded Mark of an old horse with a hat on, showed a touch of roan in his cheeks and produced the tag end of a chunk of Brown's Mule. He looked at Mark grimly. "Maybe I just don't like riots," he said, and Mark laughed.

The new sheriff hooked a hip on the edge of Rainey's desk and chewed his cud awhile in silence. "I've put your bronc around back. It's a tolerable short ride an' if you don't waste your start you can be at the border come daybreak."

"You'd like that, wouldn't you!"

"Makes no difference to me." Fraesfield's eyes rummaged his face. "Feelin's runnin' pretty strong. Word's got around we picked you up in them cottonwoods, an' why. But it's your neck, Dawson. I got just one flea to put into your ear — when you leave this town don't come back."

Mark wasn't running.

In the first place he hadn't done anything to run for and he sure wasn't letting a dirty frameup scare him out. If Journigan figured a smirched reputation and the ire of a bunch of outraged weedbenders were going to be enough to take care of him, he was likely to discover he was in line for a pair of glasses.

After leaving the flats around Blossom the trail to Muleshoe led through twenty miles of rolling prairie into a country of gravelled ridgetops, eroded gulches and mesas. Mark had come through these in the early crispness of morning and was well into the western footslopes of the Pinaleno Mountains when he came into Eph's wire.

He hardly noticed the fence at first, being much too taken up with thoughts of the curvaceous Lyla. But when he started up the round-knobbed hill across which Muleshoe had stretched this fence he came to a violent stop and stared, speechless. The five-strand fence for as far as he could see in either direction had been maliciously uprooted, and the closer he got to it the more grimly forbidding became the expression around his mouth. Some of the posts held the plain sign of axeheads. Many were broken and the few still embedded leaned crazily askew. Without quitting the saddle he could see where the wires had been cut in a dozen places, the slashed lengths snagged and tangled in greasewood.

His bleak glance, sweeping the ground, picked out the marks of shod hoofs. He found the tracks of bunched cattle traveling west at full gallop, and the look of his eyes turned brightly wicked.

There was a gate not far off but he was in no mood to hunt it. He put his horse across the cut wire and lined out for headquarters, not pushing the roan but trying rather to sort out in his mind if this were the work of nesters or rustlers. Cow thieves weren't in the habit of making extra work for themselves but in the present situation who could say what they would do; they'd have pretty easy pickings if a full-scale war broke out. Mark didn't think they'd be averse to helping one along. They might even, he thought darkly, be recruited from disgruntled nesters.

The only fact he could feel sure of was that Muleshoe cattle had been choused through that gap. And whether this stock had been stolen or scattered he did not imagine they could look for much help from Dink Fraesfield. The sheriff would give Eph a shrug of the shoulders and point out they'd no right fencing ground that had been put up for farming.

Yesterday morning Mark would probably have agreed with him — in his own mind, at least. Right now he was fed up with nesters, redhaired or otherwise. He was a heap nearer seeing the cowman's side than he'd been since the government had thrown the land open. He thought with disdain a blind mule could have told you this ground wasn't fit for anything but grass roots.

The wind had got up again. The sun had no guts to it. When the buffeting gusts began to flatten his hat brim he undid his fish and struggled into it, blowing on his fists to warm them and peering at the sky like an old sea dog. He reckoned this was like to be a damn cold winter.

Occasionally he touched up the roan's gait with a rowel but mostly he wasn't noticing if they loped or merely meandered. He was deep in the confusion of a mind too crammed with the problems of recent happenings when something struck the horn of his saddle. He swayed, wildly grabbing as the horse, with a squeal, put its head down and bucked. The belated crack of a rifle slapped the hillside behind him and Mark, savagely angry, kicked the roan with his steel and, hugging its neck, drove it into a thin screen of oakbush.

The hidden rifle spoke again and Mark, raking the far slope with a furious glance, suddenly yanked his own gun from beneath its stirrup fender and with bared teeth flung his blowing horse into the open. Straight at that shaley slope he drove him, straight toward the telltale smudge of black powder that was drifting away from the rocks where a fold creased the ridge about halfway up.

There were no more reports and there was no one around the broken cup when he reached it, but he found plenty of sign and he saw where the drygulcher had fled through a crevice in the sandstone formation. It was too narrow to take a horse through.

Leaving the roan Mark plunged after him afoot, following the tortuous windings of the fault to where it came out on the ridge's farther side; but he knew before he got there he was going to be too late. Ears filled with hoof sound he came onto a bare escarpment barely in time to see the black tail and red rump of a bay disappearing into a leafy stand of scrub oak that choked the mouth of a canyon two hundred yards below him.

He sent three slugs crashing into it, more from anger than with any real hope of targeting the fellow. He stood there rigidly staring for another several moments before, wheeling disgustedly around, he retraced his way through the wind-scoured crevice and got bleakly into his saddle. Bays were common as dirt in this country, the Muleshoe remuda could have boasted anyways twenty and practically every hand in these parts had at least one in his string. And there was nothing distinctive about this one's hoof sign, no way at all of gauging the sniper's identity. The one empty cartridge case he'd found in the cup had been jacked out of a regulation .30-30.

He reached Muleshoe headquarters in the shank of the evening with the sun dropping palely behind the distant Galiuros. Smoke was coming from the cookshack stovepipe. The remuda nickered greetings from the pole corral behind it but there was no one in the yard and no one frittering around the bunkhouse. Chicken Wing, the cook, came briefly into the shack's open doorway to empty the water off his cut-up spuds. Mark rode toward the house without exchanging any words with him.

He got down beside the porch and walked around a bay horse standing there, considering its sweat-damp hide with the sour reflection that in some ways Curly hadn't changed a goddam bit.

He stepped onto the porch and went across its warped boards and put the blue knuckles of one fist against the panels, going in out of the cold when he heard the Old Man's summons. He slammed the door shut and paused tingling beside it in the bright cherry glow of the burning coals, making out Curly's motionless stance in the shadowed dimness of the room's farther end.

He took in the soft leather of benchmade boots, the leg-clutching trousers of black-and-cream check, the tooled belt fastened with its silver buckle, snug shirt of gray flannel and flowing scarf that, lightly blue, made a gay splash of color about the bull neck. Big, Curly was, and well sprung but with too great a covering of flesh on his bones, ample proof that hard work and hard riding were no longer matters which claimed much of his interest.

His face, Mark thought now, seemed even whiter than usual and that suggestion of strain he had noticed before was about the pinched nostrils, the expression of the jaw. The black mustache above Curly's mouth seemed less precise than was its habit and the gleam of his stare was strangely kin to his stiff posture. Only then did Mark notice the bruised appearance of that near cheekbone, the scuffed red look of the big man's knuckles.

Eph said from his chair, "Wasn't figurin' to see *you*. Understood you'd been jugged."

Mark got out of his slicker. "I'll put you straight on that in a moment —"

"There's a parcel of things I aim to be put straight on."

The uncompromising bluntless of the Old Man's tone pulled Mark's head around. Even seeing them together there was little enough about these two that would give a man the notion he was staring at Curly's dad. Eph Thorpe, physically, had never run to bigness. He had always been sort of sawed-off and puny, even before his accident barely coming in high heeled boots to Mark's chin. Now, stove up from that fall off the rimrock, he mostly kept to a chair, delegating his authority to the judgment of Mark and Curly. No eastern dude, taking a look at the three of them, would have any doubts but what Curly was boss. He looked the part if any man ever did.

Eph, with his ugly weather-scrinched mug, would have been taken straight off for a busted-down puncher, some old roustabout being kept on out of sentiment. Eph would likely have subscribed to this view of things himself, setting what store he did by his son. And maybe it was right that he should, as well as natural. It was Mark's experience even the sharpest of men had blind spots. He was caught dead on between wind and water when he pulled his glance around and met the impact of Eph's stare.

He was the more taken aback because it wasn't like old Eph to make snap judgments and any man, he told himself, might have stumbled into the kind of trap Journigan had fixed for him with Lyla.

"Speak your mind," he said gruffly.

"I aim to," Eph growled back at him. "Why didn't you vote the Muleshoe crew?"

"We got in late and had to load those cattle. The buyer —"

"A lot you cared about him! By God, I ain't one to throw my charities at any man, but I think I've a right to a few straight answers. What did you an' Pell's foreman tangle over?"

Mark said stiffly, "He had runnin' off of the mouth. I undertook to quiet him."

"Way I heard this thing he seemed to have it in his head you was a heap too prone to see the sorry side of cowmen."

"Amounts to that, I reckon."

Mark, returning Eph's glare through a

tightening silence, was bright enough to know he might be talking himself off Mule-shoe. He didn't let it throw him. "I told Howlett," he said doggedly, "I was backing your play regardless, but that I figured these nesters was getting a raw deal. I'm still holding to that notion."

A flickering gleam remindful of heat lightning leaped and lay down again back of Eph's eyes. "It don't sell well, that kinda guff comin' from you. When a man licks my salt I expect his allegiance."

"Any time you figure you ain't getting mine —"

"Curly," Eph said in a voice cold as gun steel, "was stuck up an' relieved of our beef money last night. I want to know why you give out we'd got to have it in cash when you damn well knew I give you orders to bank it?"

"Who says I —"

"That's what the buyer told Curly."

"Then he lied," Mark said flatly.

Eph said, "I'm wantin' to know too why you went ruttin' after a slut, leavin' Curly to collect it."

"I never asked —"

"A man with his mind on the good of the outfit don't have to be ast to step in when he's needed. That buyer was down in the

76

bar throwin' duck fits with all that cash in his pockets an' you not around an' him due at El Paso first thing in the mornin'. Tell him, Curly."

"Well," Curly said with a kind of reluctance, "no more than I'd stepped through the batwings this fellow larruped up wild like, waving his arms and demanding to be told where in Tophet you'd got to. Said he was damned if he was going to stand around with that money and watch the Overland roll off without him; so I naturally took it."

"Never struck you as queer I'd ask for all that in cash?"

"As a matter of fact, it did. But I supposed you had a reason. There was a Texan in town looking around to move some bulls and I recalled you'd been advocating the advantages of cross-breeding. Reckoned maybe you'd talked Dad into the notion and was figuring to buy up this Texican's Herefords."

"Get on with it," Mark said thinly.

"That's about it. This buyer was frothing to catch that stage, so I accepted the money and wrote him out a receipt. I had a hunch it might be smart to put the dough in Quayle's safe but, thinking you were probably around jawing with that bull man, I set out to run you down —"

"With all that cash in your pockets?"

"I didn't leave it on the bar," Curly answered, a bright edge of anger in the wheel of his glance. "If you had been on the job —" He let that go and said bitterly, "I hadn't gone forty paces when a gun muzzle jabbed me in the small of the back. An arm locked around my neck. Somebody muttered, 'Git him into the alley!' I had a bit of luck then; the guy that had hold of me slipped and I tore loose. I hope I busted his nose in — I hit him hard enough. Then the other guy fired and they both piled into me and the next thing I knew I was stretched in the trash, bleeding like a stuck pig, all my pockets pulled out and —"

"It's God's own mercy," Eph growled, "he wasn't killed!"

"You got clipped?" Mark asked, peering across the room at him. And Curly, coming forward, pulled open his shirt to disclose the tight bandage encircling his chest. "Have it looked at?" Mark prodded.

"Hell, it's nothing but a scr—" Muleshoe's manager broke off, blackly staring across the stillness, handsome features displaying the full of his affront. "Are you by any chance suggesting I might have imagined I was shot?"

Without waiting for Mark to provide a reply he got out of the shirt with a look of cold outrage. With impatient fingers he ripped the lint loose of its fastenings.

An ugly three-inch gash plowed up by the bullet was plainly discernible even from where Eph sat. Now that the wound was bared Mark showed almost no interest at all in it. He stood with face inscrutable, silently watching Curly with a deep and dark kind of wonder slowly creeping into his stare.

5

Old Eph leaned forward, gnarled fists couched on his cane's crook, pale glare beneath the ragged bristling tufts of his eye whiskers honing Mark's face like it would wear to the truth no matter how deep hidden or despicable he found it. "Well, sir," he rasped, stern demanding, "what do you have to say fer this?"

Mark, lifting his glance off Curly, gave Muleshoe's owner a thin and taciturn interest. He roiled the palms of his hands across the leather of his chaps and stood a moment idly, breaking a trail through his thoughts before he put any part of an answer into words.

He said bluntly then, "*I* never stole your money," and pushed a heavy sigh across the stillness at Curly. "How'd you find the fence when you rode in?"

"Fence?" Curly's brows pulled down like Mark was talking Greek.

"How *would* a man find it?"

"That's what I'm asking."

Curly pulled on his shirt. "I found it same as I always have. By coming up through the —"

"You came back with the crew?"

Curly eyed him a moment with a queer, searching scrutiny. "I came back by myself," he said brusquely. "Time I'd got to my feet and got out of that alley all the boys had quit town. I spent a couple of hours trying to locate those. . . . I don't know what you're figuring to build up to —"

"I'm tryin' to line up when it happened." Mark's glance swung to Eph. "It looks," he said, "like we've got into a whipsaw. Let's go over what's happened. We hit town fairly late and started loading the cattle. Lefty Red and the buyer was on tally. I didn't ask that feller for cash. It never crossed my mind he would be in any hurry. I figured to wash, shave and eat and then go round for his check. On my way over to Ching's I saw a bunch round the schoolhouse. I swung over, aiming to vote, and was told the polls was closed.

"Them nesters was in a kind of rannicky mood so I went on to Ching's, took my bath an' got shaved. After I ate — I guess it was then around seven or maybe seven-thirty —

81

I set out for the hotel to pick up that check. Crane and Howlett stepped off the porch of the Alhambra and started jawing about the election. Howlett was feelin' ugly; he didn't care for my convictions and passed a few remarks I don't aim to take off no man. Pell put his oar in. I saw the buyer. He told me he'd paid Curly.

"A little later," Mark said, "and for reasons entirely personal, I went over to a dance the weedbenders was having at the schoolhouse. I saw an old friend who knocked me down to a girl he'd been dancin' with. We tried one. When the fiddles quit she suggested we go outside and catch some air. We were under the cottonwoods when Fraesfield and Journigan stepped out of the shadows. Dink put a gun on me. The pair of them marched me off to the jug."

Mark considered. "Seems a short time before this — accordin' to Dink — some of the Muleshoe boys roughed up a couple of nesters, wrecked one of the dives and took off for home before he could lay hands on them. Acted right pleasured to get hold of me. Heap of ugly talk in the street; think pipe was laid to have me jerked out of there. Maybe Dink got cold feet. He turned me loose anyhow and advised me to light a shuck for the border."

Mark cut a look at Curly. "After you crossed our wire you hear any shooting?"

Curly shook his head.

"Don't seem like you got here much ahead of me."

"Long enough," Eph grumbled, "to wash up an' get his clothes changed." His frowning eyes whipped a look from one to the other of them. "If you got a point, make it."

"I don't know," Mark said, "what the answer is. Fence is all tore up down along our east gate, posts out of the ground and wire ever whichway. Looks like a bunch of our stuff been over it, and it looks like to me they was travelin' damn fast."

"You mean . . ." Curly's head came up in a long dark stare. "You're suggesting they spooked and went through that fence?"

Mark rasped a hand over his jaw and said quizzically, "Ever watch a cow operate a pair of wire cutters?"

Old Eph came halfway out of his chair. But his gaunt shape lacked considerable of matching his fractious temper and he sank back, bitterly swearing.

Curly's stare, coming around, was the color of obsidian. He caught his gun belt off the back of a chair and the scowl took a deeper hold on his cheeks as his intolerant glance fetched Mark into focus. "The only thing funny I can see about that is the gall of you standing there jawing about it while —"

"Going off half cocked ain't going to get those cows back. If you're honin' to go after them you better take along the crew. There was a passle of horse tracks around that wire and it's altogether possible those cattle ain't been stolen. They may have been run off in the hopes we'd go after them."

He turned to Eph. "This thing is shaping up a whole lot faster than I looked for. Somebody, seems like, is getting a mite impatient. I hadn't got far inside the fence when somebody took a shot at me. Might have been bluff. Slug struck my saddle horn. You know where that fault cuts through Bald Ridge? Remember that cup? That's where he was shooting from. Didn't wait for me to get up there. What I can't understand though is how they wrecked that fence and got clean off with those cattle between the time Curly come through and the time I got there. You don't gather a bunch like that in twenty minutes."

Mark didn't look at Muleshoe's manager but Eph did.

Curly cleared his throat. He got the scowl off his cheeks. "They'd have had more than that — probably closer to three hours. You must have hit that wire about noon," he said to Mark. "Nearer nine when I got there. I didn't come straight home."

Mark didn't mention he was kind of late remembering that. The Old Man took it up.

"Nine?" he said, staring.

"I thought," Muleshoe's manager said, "I better look around. Got to thinking about that rigged election; all the rotgut Journigan's been throwing into those plow-chasers. Lot of wild talk going the rounds last night. Didn't know our boys got into trouble in town but I figured it might not be a bad idea to make a check on our line-camps —"

"By God," Eph growled, "you musta been outa your head! You with that wound ridin' all over hell an' gone!"

"Wasn't thinking about that. I guess with me this ranch will always come first."

"Feelin' does you credit," Eph rumbled with pride like a frog in his throat, "but you got to learn to look after yourself. Hell's fire, boy, what good's the damn ranch if I got no one to leave it to? Your health's more important —"

"Anyway," Curly said, "I only got far as Hogback," and cut the back edge of his glance over to Mark. "Who have you got holding down that camp?"

Mark said, "Pop Henshaw."

"I don't know why you keep that old fool. Anyway, he wasn't there —"

"Probably out riding fence."

"Must be aiming to go clean around it then. Two horses in the corral and never a smell of hay. No water in the trough and no fire in the stove. I hunted around what time I could spare but, by the looks of those ashes, he's not been there in two days."

Mark reached for his slicker.

"Hold up," Eph said — "be dark in half an hour. No use you tryin' to hunt for him now. I'm minded to hear more about how come you wasn't around to pick up that beef money."

"I didn't suppose there was any hurry."

"And you say you never ast him to pay off in cash?"

"I never talked with him at all until I went after the check and he told me he'd already given Curly the money."

"What time was that and where'd you see him?"

"In his room at the hotel. Right after I had that set-to with Howlett."

"At the hotel, eh?" Eph looked at Curly. Muleshoe's manager said, "Had the stage left then?"

"Couldn't say. I wasn't concerned with the stage; he didn't look like he was, either. Looked like he'd been layin' down — had a paper in his fist. Room was full of cigar smoke. He come to the door in his drawers, specs on an' teeth out an' actin' considerable on the put-out side that I should be coming around to collect for that beef. He dug up your receipt and I cleared out."

Curly glanced at his father. "Sounds like somebody's handling the truth a little careless."

Eph peered up at Mark, brows pulled down and pale stare winkless. "Sounds to me like that buyer could stand a little lookin' into. I think maybe you'd better rope yourself a fresh bronc an' —"

"He wouldn't be there now," Curly said. "He's probably halfway to El Paso."

"If Mark talked to him after you did and he showed Mark your receipt it's pretty obvious," Eph said, "he'd no intention of boardin' that stage. He could have changed his mind. He could also have been lyin' to you from the start. If he's still in town I want him fetched out here."

"Doubt if he is," Mark said quietly. He was careful to keep his eyes off Curly. "Time I'd get back there'll have been three stages cleared out of Blossom's dust. If that feller was in cahoots with the pair that jumped Curly they won't be standin' around where I could get my hands on them."

Eph, scowling, chewed on his lip awhile. "What do you think, son?"

"I'd like to know more about that rock and gun artist Mark claims took that shot at him."

Eph stared, wholly still. He cut a glance up at Mark and, hauling his look back at Curly, said, "You sure ain't suggestin' Mark dreamed up that business?"

"I'm not suggesting anything," Curly growled. "But there's too many queer things happening around here and practically every one of them's hitting at Muleshoe!"

Eph looked a little shocked but he could see it, all right. He tapped the floor with his cane. With ragged brows pulled down above the glint of his eyes he stared from one to the other of them, finally saying a little gruffly, "We're all too tired an' too upset. Wild talk ain't goin' to help none. It's hard to see a year's work go for nothin' but we've weathered bigger things than the loss of a beef crop's paycheck. Let's put off talk till we've filled our bellies —"

"Putting it off ain't going to change things. That money's gone and we won't get it back. Mark's row with Howlett ain't going to be forgotten; and what will the other ranchers think about him showing up to swing the girls at a weedbender's hoedown thrown to celebrate a bunch-quitter's election to the shrievalty? I say there's more to this than we've been told and I intend to hear Howlett's side of that fracas. Mark's been queer ever since I got back. Why would Fraesfield arrest him and then turn him loose? What was he doing to get jugged in the first place?"

Eph frowned at Mark and dragged his glance back to Curly. "Reckon that wound's mebbe botherin' more'n you think?"

"There's nothing wrong with *me* — nothing a little straight talk wouldn't set right. Why don't he answer my questions?"

"Son, he told us them was all private matters —"

"I don't see anything private about being shot at with a rifle. If we got a bushwhacker inside this fence we better know it."

"Good Lord," Eph cried, "he never claimed to think that gulcher was anyone from Muleshoe! It —"

"He thinks so though or he'd have said more about it — and there's those cattle we've lost! He said one thing I'll agree with — we're damn sure being whipsawed!"

The Old Man, shaking his head, said to

Mark, "Didn't you even catch a look at that feller?"

"He had his horse staked out the other side of that fault. Time I got through it he was off in that brush about the mouth of Field's Canyon. All I can be sure of is he was usin' a .30-30."

"Him and forty others." Curly said disgustedly, "Hell, I pack one myself!"

"I know," Mark nodded; and Eph said, "Too bad you didn't think to pick up one of them shells. Might be we could of figured somethin' from it."

"If you can," Mark said, "your eyesight's better than mine."

He didn't recall shoving his nose rag in that pocket but he had to pull it out to get his fingers on the shell. His glance, going back to the Old Man as he withdrew it, caught the weirdest look he'd ever seen on Eph's face.

A sudden chill struck through him.

His stare, following Eph's to the strangely soft feel of the stuff in his hands, discovered that in place of a nose rag he had hold of Lyla's stockings, one of them dangling full length against his chaps.

Out of the stillness Curly said, "I guess that tells the story."

6

From the moment the girl refused to make any charge Dink Fraesfield knew he was between a rock and a hard place. Without her signed complaint he had no legal right to hold Muleshoe's ramrod yet he was terribly aware that if he turned Dawson loose he would have to face the fury of the man who'd put him in office. All the while Journigan was bullying the girl and all the way back to Joe Rainey's former office he thought about nothing else. By the time Journigan left him he was nervous as a cat.

No one had to tell him what Free Grass was building up to. He had known from the time they jumped Dawson in the cottonwoods what ultimate fate Journigan had in mind for Thorpe's range boss. It hadn't bothered him then because he'd figured to be covered by the girl's sworn statement; but it was something else again to let a mob string up a prisoner he had jailed without proof or warrant. Fraesfield wasn't a timid man but he wasn't a complete fool either.

Who could ever have imagined the girl would sooner see her reputation dragged through the muck than abet a deal rigged to put behind bars the man picked out by the cow crowd to rid this country of her kind of people? Not Journigan certainly, but that wouldn't stop the man from trying to go through with it. If there should be an investigation into the lynching of Dawson the neck on the chopping block wouldn't be Journigan's.

It wasn't going to be Dink's if Fraesfield could help it.

He prowled the noisy town until he located the pair who'd got this whole business started, the ones who'd brought the word to Ed. Ignoring Gunter for the moment he demanded of the other man, "You any relation to that St. Clair skirt?"

"Naw," the gaunt one answered, "she jest hired me to drive that wagon of hers out here."

"From where?"

"From College Station, Texas."

"Know anything about her?"

"Naw. Nothin' anyways that'd be of interest —"

"I'll be judge of that."

"She's a orphan. Folks was pore white trash what come into the Texas blacklands when the boom was on back there. Old man hired out as a cotton picker but drunk up ever'thin' he ever got his hands on. Girl worked in town as a hasher. Never could figger where she got her hooks on the price of that rig. I was workin' round the hotel stable. Allowed she'd give me a hundred bucks if I'd fetch her an' that wagon to Blossom."

Fraesfield worked on his chaw. He finally said to Gunter, "I'm going to turn Dawson loose. The girl's refused to make any charges against him." He could feel their eyes stab out of the darkness. "I shall warn him he had better make straight for the border."

Gunter turned and strode off, the other man following. *Like a dog,* Fraesfield thought — *like myself following Journigan.*

He went back to his office. For a considerable while he sat deep in thought and then he called in the man Journigan had given him for jailer. "Go over to the livery and get Dawson's horse. Fetch it around to the back door and go home and go to bed."

After Dawson, released, had taken his departure by way of the rear door, Fraesfield continued to huddle there, scowling across

Rainey's desk, trying to polish into shape what he would say to Ed Journigan.

He was still working on it when an uproar of shouts angrily burst through the racket of a fast-traveling horse. Involuntarily Fraesfield winced as the staccato reports of belt guns slammed through that outside excitement.

That goddam Gunter!

He'd supposed the surly numbskull would have enough sense to lay for Dawson south of town. He sank back in his chair, trying to see where this placed him and nervously listening to the fading pound of running bootsteps. A new flurry of hoofbeats rose to swift crescendo and fled into the south.

Three minutes after that bunch of riled grangers tore out of town on the tail of Rube Krieger the sheriff's door was flung open and Journigan, hatless, swarmed into Dink's office. He had to start twice before his tongue could get traction. "D-Did you let that damn Dawson git outa here?"

Fraesfield sat very still, very uncomfortable. But now that he was faced with it, now that trouble was arrived and towering visibly, monstrously over him, quietly and even with some suggestion of dignity he answered, "No. He didn't get out. I turned him loose deliberate."

"You — *what!*" Journigan sucked in a great gust of air. His shape grew enormous and the whites of his eyes, copper stained and bulbous, rolled in his head like the eyes of a stallion bronc.

Alarm roared through Fraesfield's brain like the crest of a flash flood tearing its way through a tree-choken canyon. He was petrified with it but self-preservation was a tremendous force within him and his mind rose above this paralysis of fear. Even smiling, he said, "It might eventually add up to greater advantage for us this way."

Some of the bloat left the ridges of the big man's apoplectic features. A little of the roan congestion receded like the color in a thermometer's tube toward the Adam's apple bobbing above his askew tie. A hand tugged at his collar. "You can grin!" he growled incredulously.

"I can," Fraesfield nodded, "when I come onto something funny. Wait now — let me finish. I knew I couldn't hold him without no charge from the girl. I got to thinking. Anything happened to a feller in his position — to Eph Thorpe's range boss — might bring on an investigation that would knock your plans hell west and crooked. We couldn't afford no lynchin', but if Dawson was to get killed outside of town our skirts was reasonably clear I figured. So I got hold of Gunter and that fool who drove the girl's wagon and told them frank I was going to have to turn him loose.

"They bungled it, I reckon. May work out even better. If Dawson *does* get clear he'll have no more love for nesters. He'll probably do what you been hoping he would and really crack down hard on them."

"I don't want 'em scared out!"

"They won't be scared out — not yet. Or, anyways, not many. With me in as sheriff and you backing them openly, letting them know you have complete faith in the ultimate triumph of virtue and justice, whatever he does'll just stiffen their spines. We both know the country'll lick them at the finish but they'll have their places proved up for you then, or close enough that —"

"By God," Journigan said, "you got a head on your shoulders!"

"Well," Fraesfield grinned, "I do the best I can with it. In a couple of days I'll go out to Muleshoe and demand the surrender of those boys that started that fight that wrecked Frailey's. I'll serve a summons on Eph and we'll soak him for damages. Then we'll declare his fence illegal and you can turn your homesteaders loose on his range."

"He'll kick like a Nueches steer!"

"Let him kick. If he don't put up a fight we'll tear the rest of them fences down —"

"He'll fight," Journigan said.

"Then we've got him right where we want him. Right?"

"Right!" Journigan nodded, and showed his gold teeth in a chuckle.

"And where do I stand," Fraesfield asked, "when you're top dog?"

"Man, you don't think I'd forget you? When this country's in my pocket, Dink, you'll be livin' off the fat of the land! I'll take care of you, feller —"

"Like you'll take care of Gunter?"

Journigan looked pained. "Do you suppose I class you with that kind of swine?" But under his reproach, Fraesfield noticed, big Ed's sharp eyes were bright as glass, and just as tender. "Man, you can pick any spread in this country!"

"You want to get that down on paper?"

"Surest thing you know — just remind me sometime when I ain't in such a hurry." He wheeled around and crossed to the door. "You're Number One on my list. The first man on the gravy train. When these cowmen are busted and the plow-chasers are welcomin' twenty cents on the dollar you'll see how Ed Journigan takes care of his own."

Fraesfield nodded. Who the hell did Ed think he was fooling?

Mark urged the roan gelding up the steep shaley slope following tracks he was sure had not been left by Pop Henshaw. In the first place Pop would have no reason for coming this way, but with that brush growing up yonder anyone fixing to keep an eye on that fenceline would have a nice quiet place to conceal himself and do some waiting; and he came presently to where someone had recently done that.

No clues to the fellow's identity any more than there'd been clues back at that cup below the fault, but plenty of sign. Broken sun-yellowed grass blades showed where the fellow had stretched out while he waited. And there, the marks of his bootsoles where he'd squatted, peering down through dusty foliage at the blue and silver pool below the seepage from the spring that ran cold here through the hottest days of summer. He must have known Pop's ways pretty well, Mark suspected, retrieving the brass of a .30-30 which had bounced or rolled to partial obscurity beneath the resinous green of a burro weed.

He turned the cartridge case over very thoroughly in his hands and stepped back to the roan for his rifle, afterwards folding right knee and both bootsoles into the evidence left on this ridge. With left elbow on knee he snugged the butt of the Remington against his right shoulder and peered through the sights with finger wrapped around the trigger.

What he saw down the barrel explained Pop's absence from camp, confirming earlier suspicions without giving Mark the answer to the old man's present whereabouts.

He climbed back into the saddle and with the Remington across the pommel rode down to the fence and along its glistening wire till he came up to the shallow pool. He saw the old man then, lying face down in two feet of water. Tracks sunk into the earth's moist surface showed how the Muleshoe rider had been dragged to his present location.

Mark sat a long while looking down at those tracks and finally, sliding the rifle back into its scabbard, aimed the roan the other way and rode off along the fence in the direction of the Hogback linecamp.

It was noon with a pallid sun overhead and an increasing chill in the wind off the ridgetops when Mark reined up before the shack Pop had occupied. He fed the penned stock and adjusted the float in the horse trough and then, carrying his rifle, stepped inside the line rider's shanty.

The first thing he examined was the ashes in the stove. His bleak look had in no way lessened when he replaced the lid and stooped to squat beside the wall, narrowly eyeing the film of adobe dust which had settled over the floor. When nothing it held remained hidden he straightened and, keeping away from the room's empty middle, walked around to the table set against the far wall. No dirty dishes on it. Nothing but a little dust, and hardly enough to be sure of that until Mark dragged a finger across it.

His mind pictured Eph and his thinking went down a gray and dismal spiral to the bedrock of knowledge this trek had forced upon him. Henshaw's body had not been thrown in that sump with any idea of attempting to hide it; it had been put under water to keep the buzzards from gathering. A nice distinction perhaps but a man could guess the answer; it dovetailed with the dust in this place and the evidence of day-old ashes in the stove.

Why had Curly lied?

7

Old Eph rode at anchor in the big chair by the fire with a cold pipe clutched forgotten in his fingers and heard Muleshoe's crew come trotting into the yard. Lemon shafts from the near-down sun cast reaching purple shadows across the buff-and-black rug beyond the undraped window, and he was staring at these when Curly's boots thumped the porch boards and Curly's hand flung open the door.

Cold air, rushing in, flapped the sleeves of Eph's thin shirt against his shrunken arms. Chicken Wing, the cook, padding in from the rear, laid fresh wood on the fire, and not until he'd gone did Curly open his mouth. "We're out seventy-odd head," he told his father harshly. "Better than seventy head and not one blessed thing to show for it."

The Old Man continued to stare into the shadows.

"Seventy!" Curly said like it hacked him.

"We never even came up with a solitary cow or so much as a guess about where they've all got to!" He stamped over to the window, pulling off gloves and coat. "They went into those roughs — up there in that brush the other side of Fort Grant — and never came out. Not a scratch on that ledgerock — not a damned sign beyond it!" The man's head twisted around, his intolerant glance finding Eph. "By God, sir — are you listening?"

"You think they've been stolen?"

"Of course they've been stolen — cows don't hide their own tracks!" He put his back to the window and faced Eph bitterly. "You asked what I think. I think homesteaders got them. And I think they were helped by someone right here on Muleshoe."

Eph's glance came up briefly and then went back to the Navajo. "That's strong talk, son."

"I know it is. I hate to think, bad as you do, Mark's thrown in with that crowd, and I'm still hoping he hasn't. But I am not a total fool. This isn't a thing I like to bring up, sir, but facts are facts. Consider what's happened. What else can you think?

"According to that buyer he asked for payment in cash. He got in a fight over nesters with Jugwagon's range boss. He took a nester's woman to that weedbender's hoedown, got her out in the brush and was picked up by Fraesfield.

"Now I heard of no rumpus while I was in town but, according to Mark, some of our boys got in a brawl with some plow-chasers and left a couple of them the worse for wear. Lefty Red, when I pinned him down, agrees they did. Under the circumstances I would think we could look for Journigan to make an example of Mark, or damn well try to. On the contrary, Fraesfield turns him loose."

The Old Man's bony frame looked deeper settled in the chair.

Curly scowled, staring down at his fists. "He comes in the next night — and should have been here by noon — with a kind of unlikely tale about what's happened to that east fence. Tosses us a yarn about somebody trying to drygulch him. Even for me, that's always thought of him like a brother, that's a little bit hard to swallow."

Eph's faded eyes regarded him. "Go ahead and speak your piece."

Curly got out the makings, carefully fashioning a smoke. He took the drawstrings from his teeth and ran his tongue across the paper. "I guess I've said enough. After all, the man isn't here, Dad."

"Good time to get it off your mind." Eph tightened his grip on the crook of his cane, morosely staring into the flames. "Reckon there's a lot we don't know about him, what he got from his folks, the things that pass through his head. Environment can't do everything. What's bred into a man will show, give it time."

"That's just it," Curly growled. "Makes me feel kind of heartless, throwing the hooks into a stray. I could be all wrong. All I've actually got is some damn dark suspicions fed on things I've picked up since I got back from school. Occasional words he's let drop; funny tones, funny looks." He threw out his hands. "Not the kind of thing you can indict a man on."

"The money's gone," Eph said, "but I haven't forgotten it."

"I reckon it *could* have been that buyer."

"I understand the facts of life. There ain't none of us perfect. Git on with it, son."

"There's a few odds and ends you might not know. Like his ways with women — I've covered a lot of things for him, always hoping he'd grow out of it. I suppose what he has come to is as much my fault as anyone's. Instead of condoning these things . . . but it's done now, I reckon. I knew a long time ago how he was about money, the Indian way he nursed grudges, that predilection he has for doing his chumming with the wrong kind of people.

"I was away, of course, when the Association picked him to rod your squabble with these hoemen. Knowing Mark as I did I should have written you then; but I kept hoping the responsibility would make out of him the man you always believed he was.

"I see now how wrong and weak that was. I realized it when I learned he was fooling around with that woman. She's probably hounding him for money. The part that really sticks in my craw, though, is that business of our fence — the way he made off with those cattle; that lousy yarn about being bushwacked. A .30-30, he says, and a bay bronc's behind! Why, the whole incredible thing was trumped up to account for his time — for the time he spent rounding up that stock and jerking down fence!"

Eph sat with his thoughts, gnarled hands on his cane's crook, knowing the hell of misplaced trust, of a love that was worse than wasted. It was hoof sound entering the yard again that pulled the stubbled chin off his chest and the too-bright glance off the leap of the flames.

He kind of sighed. "We'll give him a little more rope, son."

Curly searched Eph's eyes. "Well . . ." he said doubtfully.

Mark's spurred boots made a clatter on the porch. Through the window Curly saw him and folded his lips across his teeth. Cold air came in when Mark opened the door. Curly dragged a chair toward the fire and kept standing, darkly digging at Mark with an edge of his black and not satisfied stare. Mark's own glance, inscrutably touching him, moved on to Eph. He said bluntly: "I found him."

"Well?" Eph grumbled finally.

"In two feet of water with a bullet through his back."

Eph's jaws showed twin ridges of muscle. He didn't speak, nor did Curly; but the stab of their eyes targeted Mark with questions.

"Another brass cartridge case. Same kind of gun that threw those potshots at me. I rode on to Pop's shack and warned the boys at Flint and Rawhide." His glance crossed to Curly. "Any luck with those cattle?"

"They were stolen, all right. We didn't come up with them. We lost their sign in the roughs the other side of Fort Grant."

"You talk to the troopers at the post?"

"They didn't know anything." Curly looked at him bleakly. "Seventy head," he said and, twisting his face around, spat into the fire.

Eph said to Mark, "You didn't find any clues?"

"If you want to look, I'll tell one of the boys to drive you over in the mornin'."

"If there was anything to see you'd have seen it," the Old Man said. "What are you going to do now?"

"I'm going to town," Mark said, "and report it to Fraesfield."

Curly said bitterly, "And have him laugh in your face?"

"He won't laugh."

"He won't do anything, either."

"Did you tell him about that money?"

Curly spat in the fire again.

"All right. I'll tell him about that, too." Mark buttoned his jacket and picked up his hat.

"You better eat first," Eph said. "Association's sent me word they're having a meetin'. Tomorrow, at the hotel, after noon grub. Better plan to drop in."

Mark, with his hand on the door latch, nodded. "And," Curly added, tucking it in as Mark opened the door, "don't forget where you belong."

8

After shaking the sodbusters who imagined they were chasing Mark out of the country, Rube Krieger cut back through the hills and, close to dawn, rode onto the claim he had staked in government graze which had once been a part of Pell's Jugwagon range. He fed his work stock and made sure they had water. Then he came back and looked at the horse he had borrowed. It went against his grain not to do something for it but he couldn't afford to have the animal found here. Turned loose, still unfed, it would probably go home.

He looped the reins over the horn and slapped the horse on the rump, waving his hands and shouting at it. After the horse had gone Rube went into his cabin, made a fire and reboiled a pot of warmed-over coffee. He thought of many things while he drank it, and then he rolled into bed with thoughts of Lyla and slept.

It was nearly dark again when he awoke. The drab room was filled with thickening shadows and his penned-up horses were nickering for attention. He pulled on his boots and rinsed his mouth from the bucket. Built up a fire and put the coffee pot on and went out and did his chores. He was scowling when he came back in, still thinking of Lyla and pawing through his notions. "A man ain't cut out to live alone," he told the fry pan.

He cooked and ate his supper but the food didn't set with any pleasure on his stomach. By Judas, a woman was what he needed! A strong enduring woman who could furnish his thoughts with something to bounce off of; who could take care of a garden patch, cook his meals. A woman could do a heap of things a man would never bother doing for himself. Rube wasn't thinking about keeping his bed warm, though he liked the feel of that thought too. He was just damn tired of being around the place by himself.

He rolled and smoked a dozen quirleys and, by the time he'd finished the twelfth one, he had convinced himself he'd got to make a trip to town. He put on a jacket to keep off the night chill and sloshed on his hat and went out and looped a leadrope about the neck of one of his work team. He'd left his Sunday horse and Hamley saddle at the livery, and this was his excuse for an eight-mile ride through the windy dark. Man couldn't afford to board a horse out for long.

It was around ten-thirty when he picked up the lights of town. He cut over into the tarpaper section, persuading himself it would be an act of Christian friendliness to drop by for a few minutes and see how Lyla was managing. But there weren't any lights in her shack when he came to it.

Probably pounding her ear. He hadn't figured on that, but he guessed rising eleven was pretty late for an alone woman — *if she was alone,* he thought dourly. He stirred restively on the hard ridge of his horse, not wanting to go and yet not wanting either to make any move which might culminate in proving his uncomfortable suspicions justified.

In the end he turned away without even dismounting. He made his way through back lots to a straggly clump of chinaberries at the rear of the Stars & Bars, there tying his horse and prowling afoot to where the mouth of this alley gave into the wind-swirled dust of Blossom's main drag. Quite a number of places still appeared to be open but didn't look to be doing any great amount of business. The whole burg, Rube reflected, looked like something spewed up by a drunk and forgotten.

In a way, however, he was just as well suited. Might be smarter, he figured, to get his horse and go home. He was still of this opinion when he got to the livery. Then again he got to thinking he ought to have a talk with Lyla, kind of see how she stood on the subject of double harness. By the light of the lantern hung over the door he saw old Deef Whintlace half asleep on his keg and, stepping past the man without rousing him, Rube climbed into the loft and bedded down for the night.

Long before Old Man Whintlace was up the next morning — and he was still an early riser despite his rheumatics — Rube had fetched in his work horse and given him a feed. He was currying the boarder when Deef came limping to do up his chores.

The old man looked surprised and didn't beat around no bushes. "You ort to hev better sense than show your mug around here, boy. This town ain't about to build no monument to you."

"Never expected no monument," Rube grinned.

"By grab, it's no laughin' matter! Never mind that brush; you git aboard that hoss an' git out of here quick!"

"What have I done now?"

"You'll find out, by godfreys! Just let 'em clap eyes on you an' half this town is goin' to reach for their hardware."

Rube's homely face didn't quite lose its grin but his weather-scrinched eyes turned suddenly watchful and thoughtful. "Turn it loose."

"Dink Fraesfield come over here yesterday mornin' demandin' to see every nag on the premises. He wasn't ackshully frothin' at the mouth, you understand, but some that come with him might just as well've been. They've got it in their heads you pulled 'em off on a wild goose chase. Seems like Joe Scantlin, about the time some feller was liftin' hell off its cornerstones here the other night, had his bronc stole. Sheriff's got it figured you're the one what done it, an' right now he's feelin' ringy. If you don't want to wind up in that free lunch he's just took over you better pull your freight — an' fast, boy!"

"They can't prove a thing."

"They ain't lookin' for proof right now, they're lookin' for you. Roll your hoop before it's busted."

Rube camped with his two horses in the

willow breaks north of Whitehouse Creek. He got there without discovery and spent the long hungry day shacked up in its shadows, recurrently considering whether to go and face the music or leave well enough alone. He didn't go, however, until the stars were bright above him. Then, leaving his work horse tied in a thicket, he set out once again to find Lyla.

It was late when he reached town because, against every inclination, he had used extreme care, both on the trail and during the roundabout approach to his objective. Tempered with a leavening of tolerance for other men's rights and cross-grained purposes, he yet held in large degree a cowman's contempt for the rank and file of those who followed the plow for a living. He'd linked hands with them, wanting ground of his own, but had been unable to divorce this concept, holdover from the years he had ridden for Eph Thorpe. The creep and crawl of his care came not from knowledge of their temper but from his own abiding distaste of being placed in a position where he might have to kill one of them to keep on living himself.

Rube didn't want to have to kill anybody. Thus it was well after two by the wheel of the stars when he came up through the trees and saw the shape of Lyla's shack blue and silver in the moonlight.

No shine of lamp came out of it nor had he imagined to find her up at this hour. The back yard was bright, the front deep in shadow; and this applied also to the jerrybuilt pair of shacks next beyond it. Rube quit the saddle eighty yards away, minded to see her come hell or high water. He had no wish, however, to give her neighbors any additional cause to put stock in the stories spread by Journigan's understrappers after Fraesfield's arrest of Mark; for this reason he redoubled his caution, keeping within the compass of the oaks, moving only where the murk was nearly thick enough to cut as he circled the shack's side to come at it from the front.

He was still in the trees, twenty feet from its corner, when he heard the unmistakable sound of an opening door. Frozen in his tracks Rube heard the sound repeated and understood the same door had just been carefully closed. Through a welter of clamoring questions his mind tried to tell him there were two other shacks from which the sounds might have emanated, but the strain which had hold of him did not relax.

He caught the stealth of cautiously placed boots moving toward him and the shape of a man appeared in brief silhouette against the shack's moonlit side. Recognition was instant and, deep within him, Rube cursed.

In the early evening of this night, shortly after Mark had quit the house, Curly said to his father out of an insufferable quiet, "You'll probably be glad to know I'm going to marry Rosemary Pell."

He wondered in the continuing stillness if the Old Man had heard him and was about to repeat it when Eph pulled himself out of his abstraction to stare across the room at him.

"I guess," Eph said, "you know I've always thought a heap of her."

"Thrown in with what we've got here when her old man goes up yonder, Jugwagon's range will make Muleshoe the greatest ranch in Arizona," Curly said with considerable satisfaction, and went on in his thoughts to expand this pleasant prospect. Then a shadow crossed his glance, like smoke, and he got up out of the chair he'd slumped into and went across to the sofa and picked up his coat. "I think I'll sit in on that meeting myself."

"What for?" Eph said.

"A man's got to live with his neighbors and I don't want mine getting settled in the notion this whole outfit's like its ramrod."

Eph chewed his lip and said, "You'd better stay here. This country knows where the Thorpes stand regardin' nesters."

"It may not know where *I* stand. Four years is a long time to be out of circulation. Lot of people may be thinking those years at college have changed my views. I've got to get reacquainted and it's time I was taking a hand in things, holding up my end of our responsibilities."

"You're wanting to go in on account of Mark."

"If there's to be any more of his shenanigans I aim to be where I can personally observe them."

"I don't want any trouble between you two —"

"There won't be any trouble unless he starts it."

"Look," Eph said. "There's a better way to get at this. I'll write that buyer a letter —"

"We don't know where to get hold of him."

"His firm will know."

"He's not with Betts now. He's branched out on his own. Said so the other night. Only way we can get in touch with him is to sit on our thumbs till he comes back next fall. By that time, if Mark is bent the way I think he is, we could both be in the poor-house."

He put on his coat and retrieved his hat. "I'll give him time to get on his way; then I'll take that short cut over the Pass — get a line on what's brewing before he shows up."

"That's a bad trail at night, son."

"Moon will be up by the time I ride out on the rims of those gulches. I'll be all right."

Eph fingered his stick. "Don't do anything brash." His bleak glance was as brightly unreadable as the pair of glass disks thumbed into the head of the antelope mounted over the desk shoved against the west wall. Now, abruptly, worry looked out of it and the presence of that worry was as plain in this room as the cry of the lifted wind round the eaves. "Don't let this come to a shootin', son. If Mark has turned crooked —"

"I can handle a gun a damned sight better than he can," Curly gruffed, and went out, letting the door slam behind him.

A wildness drifted with the sough of the wind and Rube with clenched fists tried to shake the weird feel of it and could not put away the awful darkness inside him. He could not reach out and find one single straw of comfort. Everywhere he looked in his mind was solid blackness, and the sound of that shape's flapping garments as, leaning into the gusts, it disappeared among the trees, was like an overture to what this country was headed for.

He swore again and let the wind push him into the solid gloom clotting the front of Lyla's shack and stood there bitter moments while his experience tried to persuade him there was nothing for him here. But a punishing desire to know the truth put his hand upon the latch and the flimsy door swung inward. Bed wood screaked and in the blue light coming through the room's side window he saw the girl come onto an elbow. He heard her gasp: "Who's there?" and caught the glint of the pointed pistol he'd loaned her; and he wanted to curse again but only groaned.

"Rube?"

"Yeah. Rube," he said, and came in and shut the door, blackly wondering who had shared that bed with her last night. He stood glowering down at her with the nails of clenched fingers biting into his palms. "What was that stinker doin' here?"

"None of your business —"

"Then I'll make it my business!"

He came nearer the bed and she threw

back the blanket, thrusting feet to the floor, dragging the hem of her shift down across bare legs. And hung fire there a moment, widely watching him, frightened.

"If you don't want company why don't you lock the door? Who else you expectin'?"

Color darkened her cheeks. She remembered the gun then and jerked it up so that the snout of it covered him, steady, unwinking, like the eye of a bull. "You've no right to come in here and — and . . ."

Rube was suddenly ashamed of himself. Then a blacker rage raggedly tore through his arteries, rowelled by thoughts of what he had seen. "By Judas, you better start talkin'. What was that polecat doin' here?"

"Why didn't you ask him?"

"I don't want no trouble with a skunk of that stripe. I'm askin' *you* —"

"You talk like I was married to you! Well, I ain't and I'm not about to be, either; I'm goin' to marry myself into Muleshoe, mister. Now take your questions and your dirty suspicions and light a shuck outa here before this thing goes off and busts a hole big enough to drive a six-hoss hitch through!"

Rube's jaw sagged. His knotted fists unclenched and fell limp at his sides. A ludicrous expression suddenly twisted his face and he cried, "Lyla girl — you don't mean it!"

"Rattle your hocks or you'll darn well find out."

"But — Hell's fire, that's crazy! He wouldn't marry you!"

"That's what he just told me. It won't be the first mistake he ever barked his shins on. What the devil do you reckon I come out here for? To get choused off like a dang muley cow?"

She pushed the hair off her cheek and glared up at him scornfully. "A lot you know about women — or him either."

She shoved her toes into slippers and slapped across the bare floor to a commode decorated with a basin and pitcher. Moonlight silvered the cracked mirror above it and she peered into this a long couple of moments, then picked up a comb and ran it crackling through her mane. "But he'll find out!" she said grimly.

She swung abruptly around and stabbed the pistol's snout at him. "How many times you think I'm aimin' to tell you? Make a noise like a bird and fly outa that door. I've had all the tomfoolery I'll put up with for one night — *git!*" she growled, scowling.

Looked like she meant it. Rube backed away from her. His shoulders felt the door.

He was twisting around to pull it open when his turning glance encountered a sheaf of crisp banknotes laying on the table.

"Judas Priest!" he cried, startled, and caught them up in shaking fingers, eyes popping as he riffled their ends in the moonlight. A low whistle escaped him. "What the hell *is* this?" he growled, eyeing her, furious.

"Just what you think it is — money," she said.

"I'm not blind! Where'd it come from?"

"I won't tell you —"

"You don't have to! That bastard Curly left it there! The price of your sin!" he flung at her bitterly.

Lyla shook the red hair back away from her face.

"Can you deny it?" he cried.

She said with curling lip, "I'll not be fool enough to bother."

Rube's shoulders sagged against the door. A groan squeezed through his teeth like mud coming out of an impaled worm. He felt sick in his guts and was fumbling blindly, trying to find the latch, when the rest of the story put fire in his wounds.

"Make no mistake. What he got," she said, "I gave him free. I should of guessed that last night in Texas, but I reckoned it were love, the measure of his concern for me. He was wild when he found I'd come here. I suppose he allowed I'd creep off like a cuffed cur dog. He come slippin' round tonight and throwed that money in my lap. Getaway money," she said, coldly angry — "get away and keep away."

She pushed Rube aside and yanked open the door and pitched Curly's bribe out into the night. "That's why I'm goin' after Muleshoe, mister."

Rube was shaking all over. "I'll ram it down his goddam throat!"

9

The Alhambra's lights were like a cluster of jewels among the moonbathed ranks of Blossom's buildings when Mark, on the roan, at last turned into the street. No other light showed except a murky glow from the smoke-filled lantern hung over the livery's cavernous door. All else was shuttered, locked up for the night, for Mark had taken his time on the long ride in and there was now little more than an hour before dawn.

He was cold and stiff from the wind and from riding but his weariness came from too much thought, thought which hadn't actually changed a damned thing. He still didn't know what he would do about Curly; the only thing he had proof of was Curly's desire to get rid of him which was wholly understandable in view of Mark's suspicions. Suspicions were one thing, proof something else. And even if he had all the proof in the world he couldn't break Eph's heart by telling him the truth.

Mark wasn't at all convinced he'd even glimpsed the truth himself yet. He strongly suspected Curly's yarn about the holdup. From its appearance he thought the gash shown by Curly in support of that story had not been achieved either at close quarters or from a belt gun; and he could not keep from dismally wondering if it hadn't been Eph's son who had put Pop Henshaw into that water.

It was a hell of a thing to think about anyone, but how near did a man get actually to knowing another? Sometimes you believed you could sense and correctly gauge another's innermost promptings but were you ever rightly able? Could you determine what forces operated to urge a man toward this or that, to bend a man like Curly — with all he had laid up for him — into black deceit and treachery? A man was actuated by a whole range of conflicting emotions, each of them pulling him in different directions. But what was the melting point or ingredient, the thing which fused or crystallized all these conflictions into character? Which made himself and Curly, once so close in everything, now so totally different?

Mark had no answer. In the final analysis

he could not believe Eph's son would do murder. He could not conceive a situation where Curly would feel driven to resort to anything so drastic. And so was faced again with his unanswerable questions. Yet Curly, when pushed into a corner by Mark with the time element, had admitted going to Pop's shack. Why had he gone so far out of his way? Certainly not for the flimsy excuse he had given. Why had he lied about conditions at Hogback? Had Henshaw been at the shack? Mark felt practically certain Curly had lied about the beef money.

Mark's lips clamped solidly shut. He could settle one part of this in mighty short order.

In pursuance of this thought he started to head for Doc Kinsley's. But almost at once he remembered that Doc, when in town, liked to eat of a morning at Lang's Oyster House and could usually be found there at 6:55. He twisted a look at the sky and wheeled the roan toward the down-at-heels courthouse. The left wing of this clapboard structure housed the jail and there was a light now in Fraesfield's office.

It never occurred to Mark that he should keep away from Fraesfield. Too many other thoughts were crowding his mind to leave room for recollections of anything so trivial.

125

Sliding down, he tossed his reins across the tie rail, tiredly climbed the six steps and pushed open Fraesfield's door.

The sheriff, frowningly going through a batch of dog-eared dodgers, annoyedly pulled his chin around and went stiffly still. His glance dropped to Mark's middle and came up with a brightening belligerence. "I thought I told you to stay away from this town?"

"Pop Henshaw's been drygulched. I figured you'd want to look at him."

"Where'd it happen?"

Mark, saying nothing about what he'd discovered at Pop's shack, related Curly's story of finding the place abandoned and wound up with an account of locating the body.

"Did you move it?"

"I didn't figure you'd want it moved." He laid a brass cylinder on Fraesfield's desk. "There's the shell that did the work. We've had a fence ripped down —"

"I should cry about that?"

"— and lost seventy-odd head of cattle; Thorpe figures they were stolen. Goin' home the other evening somebody with a rifle tried to knock me out of the saddle — happened inside our fence. You'll likely want that shell, too." He placed it beside the other. "Could be the same gent."

"Got any basis for that?"

"I don't think two bushwhackers got inside our fence."

"What you think don't concern me. My business deals with facts."

Mark indicated the cartridge cases. "You've got all the facts I was able to pick up."

Fraesfield clinked the shells in his palm. "I'll look into it." He considered Mark a moment. "I don't think, if I was you, I'd hang around any longer than necessary."

"What you think don't concern me. Better stick to your facts."

"When I've latched onto the facts I'm huntin' you better make sure you're a long way from this place."

"I've heard the wind blow before," Mark said, and turning on his heel, tramped out of the office.

He spat with distaste as he got into the saddle. Reining his horse around, he headed for the restaurant. It was in a two-story frame, the upper floor of which served as combination quarters and office for old Eph's attorney, Lefe Struthers.

Three stools were being warmed at the counter but Kinsley's rump wasn't holding down any of them. Mark inquired of the waitress who came to take his order. She glanced up at the clock. "Little early yet. He doesn't usually get in for another ten minutes."

Mark climbed onto a stool and rested his elbows. He paid no attention to the other three, who were townsmen. When his food came he went to work on it. He was mopping up the last of his egg when the door skreaked and banged and, looking around, he saw Kinsley.

"Hi," Doc said. "How's things out at Muleshoe?"

Picking up his cup Mark moved away from the counter. "Let's set over here." He led the way to a table at the far side of the room. Doc sank into a chair, stretched his face in a yawn. "I don't know why the hell I get up so damn early. You been having trouble out there?"

"We ain't been havin' no picnics." Keeping his voice down Mark described the loss of the beef money, told of the fence and cattle and concluded with his discovery of old Pop Henshaw's body.

Doc shook his head. "Why would anyone kill a harmless gaffer like him?"

"I can't figure it," Mark said. "It's gettin' so I can hardly tell up from down." He'd been hoping, while recounting Curly's story of the holdup, Doc would come out with some remark about Curly's wound; but, since he hadn't, Mark said now, like it wasn't no more than the tag-end of a passing thought, "I don't suppose he'll have to worry about that bullet gash gettin' infected?"

"Hard to say, not having seen it. Whereabouts did this bullet catch him?"

"Across the ribs. I expect —"

"If it was much of a hurt I don't guess he'd have ridden clean out to the ranch without having it looked at."

Not if he'd got it here, Mark thought. He tossed off his coffee and put down his cup. "I better get at my errands. Association's holdin' a meeting this noon."

Doc signalled the hasher. "Another discussion of the homesteader menace?"

Mark grimaced. "I reckon."

"You watch out for those buggers."

It was an overcast day with clouds hanging heavy as boiler plate above the dust-strewn flats taken over by these farmers, and Mark glanced up anxiously as he stepped into the saddle. Plow crowd, he reckoned, would be praying for rain. Might get some yet but it looked more like snow. He turned up his coat collar. Felt like it, too.

He sat a moment trying to get his thoughts together, trying to stack up in his mind the chores that couldn't be put off. The most important thing was that meeting, though he expected he could name right now what it was called for. Pell would be wanting to chew the tail off him for not cracking down a whole heap harder on these weed benders. There wasn't much patience in Pell, Mark reflected; he was a man who craved action and it would go almighty hard with any man who had the temerity to put a plow through his grass.

He remembered then, Mark did, he had forgotten to tell the sheriff about the loss of that beef money. He had told Eph he'd report it, and he guessed he had better go do it before his mind got him sidetracked with further visions of Lyla. It shamed him to keep thinking of her after the way she'd used him. *I ought to have more damn pride,* he thought, but everywhere he looked he found her face and shape still in front of him.

He turned the roan around and started him moving toward the courthouse. Lyla's stockings were burning a hole in his pocket and memory of her lithe resilience, like the taste of her lips, was in his blood like a virus. He was hating himself when his glance fell on Rainey coming toward him with a blanket rolled back of his cantle.

Mark pulled up his horse. "Where you off to?"

"Just as far as I kin get from this gone-to-hell place."

"Shucks, it ain't that bad, is it?"

The ex-lawman's lips pulled away from his teeth. "I've outlived my time around here by the looks."

"Eph would probably —"

"I'm not askin' for charity and I'm too old to ride rails." He considered Mark bleakly. "You're a fool if you go near that meetin'. Pell's out to nail your hide to the fence."

"Nothin' new about that —"

"There's a lot new about it! Don't you know, by God, there's no place here for honesty?"

Town's noises came through the gray light strangely muted. The rain call of a crow lifting suddenly on flapping wings. Somewhere a child cried forlornly and from the direction of the livery came the sound of wrangling voices.

"What have you heard?"

"I suppose you know Curly's marryin' Pell's daughter —"

"Where'd you get that?"

"I got it from Pell. He spent the night here linin' things up for a showdown. I used to think I knowed these people but — Hell! A blind mule could savvy what that pair's up to. Quick's they're kinfoiks — an' that'll be Friday — they'll throw these spreads together and have the toughest pack of riders the devil ever grinned at!"

"Some time they might," Mark admitted, "but not while Eph —"

"Eph!" Rainey snorted. "Give you a string of spools, by God, and a man wouldn't know which was Thorpe and which was Dawson! When you goin' to get your eyes dug out?"

"Nothing wrong with my eyes."

"Then you must be packin' solid ivory back of 'em. There's talk been spread —"

"What talk?"

"I'll skip the woman." Rainey glared at him irascibly. "It's claimed you're takin' cowman pay and horsin' round with these nesters huntin' ways to put the cattle crowd plumb outa business. Howlett's got you workin' hand in glove with Journigan. Some of them's sayin' if this stuff ain't so how come Journigan's sheriff turned you loose the other night? Go over to the Alhambra if you want to get a earful. They're sayin' this mornin' you bushwhacked one of your own men, dammit, to give them farmers a chance to pull down fence!"

The bones stood out in Mark's face like castings.

"You better strap on a hogleg," Rainey said grimly. "Or stay on that horse and start makin' tracks."

"I'll be at that meetin'," Mark said through his teeth, "and I'll still be around when that meeting's over."

"You bet you will — too dead to skin! Well," Rainey grumbled, picking up his reins, "don't say you wasn't warned."

10

Mark heard Howlett before he got to the batwings and all the simmering frustration of the past three days boiled suddenly into a red haze of fury that took no account of odds or anything else.

The Jugwagon boss saw him coming and a shocked surprise ran over his features. The whole bottom dropped out of his talk and he went stiffly still for about a half second while his disturbed stare flashed a quick look about him. Then, reassured, confident this crowd was solidly with him, he grinned at Mark wickedly. "Ain't you kinda out of your element? I had a notion this place was reserved to cowmen."

"A snake sounds the same wherever I hear it," Mark answered, stopping three feet away from him. "Don't let me quiet your rattle, Howlett. That's what I'm here for, to get a clear load of it."

"Why, you bunch-quittin' bastard —"

Howlett swung for Mark's jaw with all the hate that was in him. Mark, ducking, came up and clipped him side of the ear. Shaking his head, Howlett leaped. Mark's left cut his wind off; Mark's right, coming up, flung him crashing against the bar. With his eyes gone berserk Howlett grabbed up a bottle. Mark kicked him in the shins and wrenched the bottle away from him. Howlett went for his gun.

Mark had no choice. He hit him with the bottle.

Howlett, screaming, reeled away but got his pistol clear of leather. Flame burst from its snout as Mark tried desperately to reach him. Mark struck the man again, drenching him with whisky as the bottle smashed against Howlett's skull. The bottle's neck, in Mark's fist, dragged a bright track of scarlet through the stubble on Howlett's face. The man staggered. His knees let go and he fell groaning by the bar. Mark stamped a boot on his wrist and came up wild eyed with the pistol.

He wheeled toward the doors through completest silence and that was when he saw Curly. He stopped. Curly's face was like parfleche. "Outside," Mark grated. "I've got something to say to you."

Curly's tongue crossed his lips, he flung a

nervous look about him. But no one offered to be helpful. "Wait," he said. "You're excited —"

"You bet your sweet life I am! Get outside them doors before I come over there and take hold of you."

Curly, reluctantly putting what grace he could on it, moved toward the batwings. Mark followed him out. When they got to Mark's horse Curly said in an affronted voice, "Was that necessary? If you had to see me right now you could at least have asked civilly."

"If you got what you rate you'd be down on that floor with Howlett!"

Curly's teeth shone with anger beneath his darkening cheeks but a view of Mark's eyes drew most of the heat from his outrage. He scowled, closed his mouth and relapsed into silence.

Mark said, "I'll take that gun belt."

Plain wickedness burned in the depths of Curly's stare but it was stayed by the glint of Howlett's gun in Mark's fist. He unstrapped the heavy belt with its shine of bright cartridges and, carefully rolling it about the scabbarded pistol, reluctantly passed it over. Mark, accepting it with his free left hand, rummaged the look of hurt bewilderment warped on the contours of Curly's face.

"I'm goin' to ask you some questions," he said thinly. "What happens after that depends a lot on what you tell me."

"You don't need my gun to ask questions, do you? I don't understand you, Mark," Curly said.

"Sometimes I'm not sure I understand myself. What'd you do with that beef money?"

Curly's gasp as he drew back to stare wide eyed at Mark was dumbfounded. He showed all the shocked innocence of a child just told about Santa Claus. "Beef money? Have you forgotten those two thugs?"

Mark's lips curled with scorn. "I haven't forgot anything." The confusion undermining him for thirty-six hours was gone now, burned away in the violence he had been through with Howlett. He was still caught fast in the trap of allegiance but for once he was seeing Curly Thorpe without blinders — seeing him objectively with all the bitterness of knowing what it was he'd got to do.

"That's your answer, is it?"

"What else can I say? You know as much as I do. You know how dark it can get around here. These two fellows came up —"

"And those seventy head of cows we lost. You're sure they was rustled?"

"Driven off by nesters. If they weren't I'll eat them!"

There were no hands left on the Muleshoe payroll that had hung up their hats during Eph's days of hiring; old Henshaw had been the last. The crew they had now was three times as efficient; close-mouthed, hard and hand-picked by Curly right over Eph's ramrod's head, Mark remembered.

"Hoofs, horns and hide?"

"Tails, too," Curly grinned, restored to good humor. He seemed more relaxed now, his handsome face very earnest, his words again packed with the ring of confidence. "It was in that brush where we finally lost them. Tracks went onto that ledge-rock —"

"And that afternoon you rode out to Hogback you never saw Pop Henshaw at all?"

"How *could* I have seen him?" An edge of testiness cut through Curly's tone. He said, abruptly impatient: "I told you how I found things. Horses penned up without feed, without water —"

"You told me a bunch of bare-faced lies. Now I'll tell you the truth," Mark said harshly. "You quit the herd early the day we rode in so you'd have time to make sure we got paid off in cash. You collected that cash and you kept it. You — don't try nothin',

Curly, or a Jugwagon bullet will fix you for buryin'."

He gestured with the snout of Howlett's sixshooter. "Just stand there while I fill in the rest of it. You stole that money. You reckoned I'd suspect and so you tried to cover up. You went down among them tarpaper shanties but you didn't waste much time once you'd got your hands on that money. You hit out for Muleshoe. You got those cattle together and you cut that fence. I think you probably talked some nesters into drivin' off that stock. But fear got hold of you. So you laid for me."

"Make it good while you're at it!"

"You had the right idea," Mark nodded, "but you was just a shade eager. When your first shot didn't drop me you spooked and tried to get out of there. You had to scramble through that fault, and when I got through all I saw was the rump of your horse. But I put three slugs into that brush and one of them come within a ace of gettin' you. If you'd got that gash the way you claimed you'd have gone to Kinsley —"

"I did. He wasn't home."

"Save your breath. It happens that canyon you rushed into comes out just west of Hogback. Henshaw either saw you there or met you comin' out of it. That settled his

139

hash. He had lint and gauze and stuff in the shack, but you didn't want him yappin'. So you sent him around the fence line, knowin' he'd drink when he got to the spring; and you laid for him on that ridgetop.

"But you weren't satisfied with that. You had to dress it up some more, tellin' me by the look of things he'd been away for a couple of days. I knew you was lyin' when I looked at them ashes."

Curly tried to laugh it off but his lips were too stiff, his throat too parched; and with his eyes the color of murder he said, suddenly livid, "You can't prove a goddam thing! You —"

"Stick around," Mark growled, "and you'll find out what I can prove. Go and I'll keep my mouth shut. But if you ain't cleared out come nightfall you're goin' to get everything you been askin' for."

It was the craziest kind of bluff, of course, his laying the law down to Curly that way — a desperately contrived bit of pure-skein hokum, predicated on the chink he had uncovered in Curly's armor and designed in the hope they might still avoid the fruition of whatever plans Curly had patched up with Pell. All too well did Mark realize he could never bring himself to the point of exposing Curly. He couldn't do that to Eph.

He prayed Eph's son wouldn't sense this. That, grasping, egotistical and self-seeking as he was, Curly would be in too much fear of forever losing Muleshoe to defy him. That fright, suggesting discretion to be the smarter part of valor, would chase Curly out of their lives for awhile.

That this at best was but the flimsiest kind of a makeshift had not stopped Mark from embracing it; better a postponement, a compromise with evil, than that they should eye each other across leveled pistols, the only other alternative Mark could latch onto. A duel might leave Curly's name unblemished but, regardless of who won, the net result would be like a smash in the face to the man who had raised and loved both of them.

Curly, following Mark's ultimatum, was in a fine sweat of fury. He could hardly breathe, so wild and violent was the chaos of his thoughts. Fright's cold thread of fear ran jaggedly through him like a hacksaw. It never occurred to him Mark was bluffing. In the range boss' place he wouldn't have hesitated a moment to do what Mark had threatened. He shook and cursed and trembled and then, about to climb the loose planking of Quayle's cracked and splintered steps, discovered Mark's incredible folly.

A grin broke through the twisted contour of his cheeks. His eyes, maliciously brightening, swept the street with a growing excitement. He loosed a chuckle deep inside him. *So that wagon train stray is going to fix my clock, is he?*

He took a look at the overcast sky and said aloud, "the righteous bastard!" Then quitting Quayle's steps, he turned quickly up an alley that fetched him around to the back of Messner's Hardware, and stepped through its rear door without knocking. He took the swivel by Messner's desk and lit up one of Messner's stogies and sat there, unseen by the store's customers, until Messner himself came into the back room to pick up something.

"I want a gun," Curly told him. "Short barrel, big caliber. A pistol I can pack in my pocket."

In a back room at the Stars & Bars three men sat around a poker table that had nothing in the way of their elbows but a part-filled bottle and three glasses. "Pop Henshaw's been killed out near their Hogback linecamp," Fraesfield said, looking at Journigan. "He brought me the news about an hour ago. That might even have been what he come for; I don't think so. But, whatever the reason, he's still around town."

Dog Town Slim, the vacationing gunman from Tombstone, poured himself another drink. "I suppose, by that, you mean he's available."

"He's here," Fraesfield nodded; and Journigan said, "There's a hell's smear of cowmen here. I tell you I don't like it! Pell spent the night here — Curly Thorpe, probably, too. Crane rode in with his boss half an hour ago. Zeigler's come in and old Ty Ronstadt from Cuero. What's comin' off? That's what I wanta know."

Fraesfield said, "Likely nothin' but another of those Association gab fests. There ain't none of the forty-dollar crowd here. I don't see no point gettin' your bowels in an uproar. Dawson's the man you're after and he's right here now like a settin' duck."

Mark, recollecting he still hadn't notified the sheriff about the alleged holdup during which Curly claimed to have been robbed of Muleshoe's beef money, spent a long five minutes trying to make up his mind whether the effort of going over there again was worth the bother. He was convinced Curly's story was built from whole cloth but he had no means of proving this and, if there was a shred of truth in it, he supposed the sheriff should be given the benefit of hearing it. There might be questions he'd want to ask while Curly was still get-at-able. In the end Mark turned his roan once again toward Fraesfield's office.

But the sheriff wasn't there.

He had a foot in the stirrup and was about to swing up when Lyla St. Clair came out of Stein's store in a Mackinaw jacket with her arms full of bundles. Almost against his will Mark lowered the foot and finally touched his hat. Her red lips tried a timid smile and Mark, leading the roan, moved grudgingly toward her.

"Golly, it gets cold here!" She regarded her breath and made a little face at it. "Reckon it's goin' to snow?"

Mark, in no mood for small talk, growled, "Nobody but a fool or a tenderfoot would try to prognosticate weather in Arizona. Give me those things you've got —"

"I can make out to tote them. They're not heavy, really."

Mark took them anyway and tied them on his saddle strings. "I been layin' off to have a talk with you." He picked up the roan's reins and fell into step with her. Someway, now, his black imaginings didn't matter and the hard thoughts he'd cherished seemed of no more importance than the rope burns he'd got during roundup. There was something about her nearness that changed the day's whole aspect.

She glanced up at him slanchways. "You still got them stockin's?"

He nodded, flushing, scowling with embarrassment. She took hold of his arm; and, hearing her throaty chuckle, he grinned a little, sheepishly. She squeezed his arm. "I'm sure goin' to need them if it keeps up like this. Goin' to have to get some firewood, too. You know where to get it?"

"Expect I could rustle some."

"You ain't mad then — with me, I mean? About the other night? I been some worried you might figure I got you out there a-purpose."

"It did kind of hack me for awhile but I got over it."

"Gosh," she said, "I didn't have no idea them fellers would foller us out there. That Journigan kind of fancies himself, don't he? Come around to my shack a-layin' the law down." She laughed, looking up at him, and said in fierce mimicry: " 'I'm big taters in this man's country — Don't figure because you're a woman you're goin' to git anywhere buckin' me!' "

Mark chuckled in spite of himself. But suddenly earnest, he said, "If that bumbershoot sets out to give you any trouble —"

"I ain't scared. If he comes snoopin' around my place any more I'm liable to play him a tune on Rube's pistol-gun. Rube says that'll learn him."

"Yeah." They strode a few steps in silence. "You're pretty fond of Rube, I reckon."

"Sure am." She twisted her head to look at him. "Rube's just like a brother."

It was ridiculous how much brighter the day looked. It did, though. Felt warmer, too; and the smell of her hair was sweet with soap and Mark was suddenly impatient to get to her shack and stretched out his legs. Half running to keep up with him, she said, "Gosh, what's bit you?"

Mark reckoned it was the love bug but he hadn't the courage to say so. "Figured you'd want to get home and get into them stockings."

"I ain't in that much of a hurry. It's kind of nice, don't you think, walkin' along just you and me this way?"

Mark nodded. "Things look mighty pretty, this time of year. You latched onto some land yet?"

"No. But I'm goin' to. I'm goin' to have me a big spread and dress like a Queen. I'm goin' to have me a carriage with red wheels and brass lamps on it, and when I drive through this burg all these folks'll stand bug-eyed. They'll say, 'Lord — there goes that Lyla! I remember her when —' " She broke off , laughing. "Does that sound crazy to you?"

"Well, no," Mark said, but he didn't do any laughing.

Lyla's face sobered too. "Ain't you never built any castles?"

"They didn't run to brass lamps," Mark said gruffly.

Her hand on his arm seemed not as tight as it had been and her glance stayed fixed on some vague place far ahead of them while an unwanted silence came and made talk impossible. He tried to tell himself it was all in his head or that the gray gloom of these trees was probably having an effect on her. Then they came out of the oaks and she let go of his arm. She said, "Here we are," in a voice that had gone a hundred miles away from him.

Mark unfastened her bundles and she pushed open the door and he carried them in and put them down on the table. His hands were numb with the cold. He said,

"I'll get you some firewood."

She turned to look at him doubtfully. "You been to enough trouble now on my account."

"I don't have to share it," Mark said irritably, and went out.

It took him longer than he'd reckoned. All of the dead wood seemed to have been gathered, probably picked up long since by other nesters quartered round here. They were like locusts, he thought, less inclined to blame Lyla for her talk of brass lamps. It was, he guessed, a symbol of better times in her thinking. He wasn't sorry he'd been short with her; with so much on his mind he didn't realize that he had been.

She let him in, not speaking, and he stacked the wood by the calcimined mud of the fireplace. She brought him the paper off some of her parcels and he got a blaze started. When he climbed up off his haunches he found her watching him unreadably.

He was surprised how clean this place was, how attractive she had made it. Some way he felt too conscious of the strangeness of his presence here, confined within four walls with her and with the contradictory urges he felt clawing for expression. He could have reached out and touched her and yet unexplainably, in his mind, he felt a million miles away from her.

He couldn't grasp the significance of this, couldn't free himself of the uncomfortable conviction she was waiting with all a weedbender's patience for him to make his goodbye and take himself off. Completely out of her life.

He dragged off his hat and stood there crazily twisting it, afraid almost to look at her although he knew very well that she was still watching him.

He finally pulled his head around and, when their glances locked, a tiny whisper of breath seemed to come sighing out of her. Without quite knowing how it actually happened she was suddenly in his arms, their mouths pressed hungrily together. For him there could never be any other woman; deep inside himself Mark knew this. Just to hold her like this dissolved all his problems in a tremendous satisfaction that was just like going through the roof of the world.

When he finally stepped outside her door he did not feel the cold wind bitterly plucking at scarf and coat collar — that flung loose grit against the legs of his Levis and whined a dirge as it fled whistling around the eaves.

He didn't see the black look of the clouds

piled above him or the drabness of his surroundings. The sky, in his mind, was a dazzling blue, new washed as though with rain and bright with the glint of sunlight. He felt seven feet tall and at the same time bashful and unbelievably tender. This mood was like nothing he'd ever encountered before. Nothing but the need of representing Eph at that meeting could have pulled him away from this cabin now.

Still lost in the wonder of his thoughts, of this good feeling, he stepped into the yard and moved across to where the roan, hips hunched against the wind, morosely stood on dropped reins. Backing the horse he picked the reins up. He pulled the slack from the fishcord cinch and was lifting a foot to settle it into the oxbow when a voice rasped sharply from the cabin's corner: "Hold it, Dawson!"

11

Doc Kinsley was not the only man who observed Mark Dawson walking away from town with Lyla. By the barrel cluttered loading dock that flanked the west side of the Stars & Bars the Tombstone gunman, Dog Town Slim, also picked up the pair; and back of the dust-streaked window of Ching's barber shop Curly Thorpe watched him, too, with eyes that were bright with desperation and malice.

Jealousy had nothing to do with Curly's feelings and under other circumstances he would have been prepared to give Mark's attention his whole-hearted blessing. In the present case Muleshoe's ramrod was the last man he cared to see in the girl's company. Up to now Mark had nothing but an assortment of suspicions. It was in Lyla's power to give the man proof, and it was in Curly's mind that she would probably do it.

He thought of waylaying them, of

shooting Mark down just like you would a mad dog; but he was shrewd enough to understand this would only be swapping the witch for the devil. If he took care of Mark personally he'd damn well better do it where that redheaded biscuit couldn't put the finger on him.

He was inclined to believe he'd be a fool to tackle personally a job he could easily hire others to do for him until he considered the stakes and perceived probable consequences. If he could keep Lyla quiet until he came into the place he could then wash his hands of her with impunity; popular prejudice would take care of Lyla. It was her threat to his plans embracing Rosemary Pell that had been most on his mind up to this point; he'd seen the need for Pell's help and marriage to Pell's mule-faced daughter looked the cheapest way of getting it.

Now, however, faced with Mark's ultimatum and with the sight of them heading openly for the girl's shack in shantytown, Lyla represented through Mark a very real and personal danger. Mark had threatened to expose him if he didn't clear out; but if he learned from Lyla about that money Curly had given her . . .

I can't risk it, he thought. *I've got to shut*

that bastard's mouth and I've got to do it pronto!

He couldn't farm it out. His experience with Lyla was a warning. He dared not put his future in the hands of a man who could hold murder over him. He would have to get rid of Mark without help unless . . .

"Goddam it!" he said, going out to his horse and climbing into the saddle. "If I could hit on some way of forcing him into a brawl with somebody else . . ." But there was no guarantee that wouldn't wind up like Howlett. Unless. . . .

Whatever he did would have to be done quick, and it would have to be final. If this deal went to pot there'd be no chance for another. He watched the pair appear again beyond the planks of the stockyards. Headed for Lyla's shack, all right. He wished he knew for sure what that son of a bitch was up to. With anyone else there'd be no need for this guessing, but with Mark — by God, you just couldn't tell!

He realized now that from the start he'd been holding this girl too lightly. He'd been a fool for grabbing that beef money, and a bigger one for imagining she could be bought off for cash. What if she went to old Eph with that money!

He'd got to shut her mouth. She'd become as big a threat to his future as Mark. He'd got to put her where she couldn't talk. Then a note sent to Mark with her name on the bottom. . . .

Curly's teeth ground together. Gunter — Journigan's man — was the fellow to get hold of. Be a goddam shame to give up a good sideline, but this was no time to be crying about pennies. The note, then Gunter, then Howlett. That would do it. Then let those wedding bells ring out!

Turning his horse to the tie rail fronting the hotel, he swung down and went in and climbed the stairs to the balcony overlooking the lobby. Here was the man to start the ball rolling. As Association president his remarks would carry a lot of weight with the cow crowd.

Exultantly Curly put his fist to Pell's door.

Reflex was all that saved Mark in that moment.

Instead of whirling or freezing in his tracks as expected, instinct dropped him like a shotgunned goose. The slug intended for his heart screamed off the cantle of his saddle. The roan commenced pitching. Mark was rolling when he struck the ground but he got a hand on Curly's pistol

154

and a faceful of grit as lead geysered dirt scant inches in front of him. Half blinded, he couldn't see the man but he jerked up the gun and, firing by sound, sprayed his shots in an arc, triggering until the hammer began clicking on empties.

Cutting into the diminishing crashes of sound Lyla's voice frantically reached him and he came up on an elbow, seeing the man's shape through the scald from the gravel. He sensed the girl beside him; struggled upright. Lyla buried her face against his chest, trembling. He put a rough hand on her shoulder, gently kneading it, talking to her like he would to a frightened horse, staring across his hand at the cold dead eyes of Dog Town Slim.

When the girl quit shaking he steered her toward the open door. "I'm not hurt," he said, handing her over the step. "Don't worry about it; it's over now."

"But Mark —" Her eyes searched his face, too large, the fear still bright in them. "You're so alone . . ."

"But I've got you to come back to. It's worth a lot, knowin' that. Chin up now," he grinned. "I'll get away just as quick as that meetin' is over." Very gently he pushed her inside. "Keep that door barred."

Crane, the Terrapin segundo, was just

155

going up the hotel steps when Mark, leaning against the push of the wind, strode past with the man lashed across the roan's saddle. Crane turned clear around, startled eyes staring after them, watching Mark stop the horse beside the courthouse steps. Untying his dead freight, Mark got the man over a shoulder and disappeared inside.

The pervading gloom of the long drafty corridor was given a hiatus by the solitary flare of a pot-bellied bracket lamp. But the dingy walls and double line of closed doors had too long absorbed the smell and tears of human misery to be much impressed with so indifferent an attempt.

At the spur-scarred desk with its frieze of cigarette burns in the office where for the past two decades the deposed Joe Rainey had shined the seat of his pants on the tax-payers' tithes, the present incumbent caught the oncoming tramp of high-heeled boots and lifted a disgusted scowl from his papers. But when he wheeled in his swivel to face the cause of this distraction what he saw in the doorway changed his look in short order.

Suspicion darkened his glance, became certainty and bulged it. His knuckles turned white in their grip on the desk edge. Mark said: "Here he is, Dink," and dumped the

156

cadaver down in a chair.

The sheriff licked at stiff lips. An oily shine filmed his cheeks and in the glow of the lamp he looked ten years older than he had two hours earlier. His mouth moved but no sound came.

Mark said cold as a well chain, "Get a warrant fixed up for the arrest of Ed Journigan."

Fraesfield cleared his throat. He seemed to have trouble getting hold of his breath.

"Right now," Mark said, and the sheriff looked sick.

He tried to pull himself together, tried to cover his fright with bluster. "Did you see Ed kill this feller?"

"Nope. I didn't see him pay this feller to kill me, either, but the money's in his pocket —"

"That's preposterous!" the sheriff said loudly. "If you gunned this man —"

"I didn't come here to argue."

The sheriff studied him nervously. His tongue crossed his lips again. "That's a pretty serious charge. I'll have to have more details —"

"If I had the details," Mark said, "you'd probably go to jail with him. Now get off your fat prat and get me that warrant."

"No jury in this county would convict

him on your say-so." Fraesfield waxed a little bolder. "You'll never make it stick —"

"It'll stick all right if the government steps in." Mark's grin was a splinter of white in the lampshine. "If I can't get him for attempted murder there's plenty of other things I can throw at him. Usin' the mails for a skin game. Taking fees for settling farmers on government land — and then not doing it. Slander. Intimidation. Stuffin' ballot boxes." He said, coldly angry, "You want to hear a few more?"

Fraesfield made one last try. "If you fetch in the government these ranchers wouldn't leave enough of you to stuff a tobacco tin!"

"But where will you be?"

"You wouldn't dare!"

"If you want to find out," Mark said, "just keep settin'."

The news flew like wildfire.

When Mark stepped into the hotel dining room his presence went unnoticed for perhaps as long as ten seconds; then, like the ripples from a rock dropped into a millpond, in ever widening circles heads began twisting. The clatter and gab fell away to dead quiet.

At the head table Pell got up onto his feet. "This meetin' is called to order!" He rapped the board with his gavel. "We're going to dispense with the minutes and all other preamble and get right down to the reason for us bein' here. As you all know, that reason is this congregation of squatters who've been fillin' the town with unrest and violence, rammin' round cuttin' fences, killin' cattle — inaugurutin' an outbreak of rustling never paralleled before in the history of this country!"

He was tall, gaunt-faced, intolerant and arrogant, proud with the pride of hard cash and vast acreage. When the growls had subsided he held up a hand. "We better hear first of all," he said, "from Mark Dawson, the man we appointed to deal with this riffraff. All right, Dawson."

There was a craning of heads again and Mark, staring into that sea of grim faces, saw men whom he knew, men he'd grown up with, but nowhere encountered so much as one friendly glance.

Pell said impatiently, "Get on with it, man. You've done some work on this, haven't you?"

"I've poked around with it a little —"

"What's the present situation?"

"Well, a few of these farmers, maybe twenty or thirty families, have been located on land which the government set as —"

"Hell's fire! We know all that! What we want to find out is what steps you've been takin' and what you've accomplished toward gettin' 'em off the county."

"If they're on it," Mark said, "I guess you know whose fault that is. You ought to kno—"

"We're not here to discuss whose fault it is! What we're askin' is *why you haven't got rid of them!*"

There were growls of grim approval from that sea of cow crowd faces. Mark recoiled a little from the solidarity of it, cheekbones paling beneath the glint of a narrowed stare. He had no doubt now of their temper. Old Rainey had certainly called the turn. This bunch was after his scalp. In his anxiety to stave off violence he had crouched too long on the top of the fence.

He didn't jump into speech but looked them over with care, hoping to find one man he could appeal to; but the longer he considered them the more bleak his own expression became. Take them individually the most of these boys were pretty good fellows but, taken in the bulk, they were tired of horsing round. Fed to the gills with nesters they were in no mood for any lecture on tolerance. They wanted an end to this worry about grass and fences. They wanted these plow-chasers out of here and by the look of their faces they were hellbent for action.

This knowledge didn't change Mark's private convictions. "I'm not here to argue the merits or shortcomings of the Homestead Act. A law can be amended but you can't put together busted hearts or sponge a feud off the slate the way you would a bunch of figures. These men may have been misguided but they came here in good faith —"

A roar of booing cut him off and put a flush across his features. With clenched fists he waited through that ugly sound and said when it subsided, "The man responsible for their being here — Free Grass Journigan — has just been locked up in the —"

"Sorry to interrupt you," the sergeant-at-arms muttered, tapping his shoulder, "but I was told that this was urgent." He held out a sealed envelope across the outside of which Mark's name had been scrawled with a pencil, and the words *Foreman of Muleshoe — personal.*

A good bit of the color went out of Mark's face and something fluttered in his stomach as he eyed the girlish character of that inscription. Stepping back, without apology, he tore open the envelope while a growl of renewed conversation sprang up and many bleak stares continued stonily to watch him. He drew out the twice folded inclosure with fingers he had to fight to hold steady. There were only seven words above Lyla's initial. *Come as soon as you possibly can.*

Crumbling the note Mark swung around to face Baiden. "Where'd you get this?"

"One of them nester kids fetched it."

Several of the cowmen sitting nearest caught the sergeant's answer and passed it, scowling, to other cowmen behind them. Pell rapped on the table. He said, when Mark pulled his cheeks around, "So Journigan's in line for eatin' out of the public's pocket. May I ask what you had him arrested for?"

"On my complaint Fraesfield has him booked for conniving at stuffing ballot boxes —"

"What the hell good will that do?" someone yelled from the rear. "That shyster of his will have him out before nightfall!"

"I don't think so," Mark said quietly. "That was only one of the things he was charged with. I don't think any shyster in this town will care to become mixed up with a man accused of using the U.S. mails to defraud —"

"This your idea of the best way to clean

them damn weedbenders —"

"Just a minute," Mark said, getting red about the cheeks again. "You don't have to use violence to get those people —"

"The hell you don't!"

The room was a racket of shouting and catcalls. Veins stood out on Pell's corrugated forehead as he angrily hammered the table to get attention. Finally, disgusted, he did some shouting of his own. "You gave the man the job! Now, God damn it, give him a chance to tell —"

"He's been at it six months and all he's done is jail that pipsqueak Journigan! Who the hell does he think he's kiddin'?"

"Lemme at the nester-lovin' bunch-quitter!"

"What's he done to get rid of them churntwisters?"

There was more of the like but Pell, catching Mark's eye during a lull in the heckling, motioned him to go on. Mark said in a mood of cold rebellion, "You boys achin' to ranch or kill nesters? If it's blood you're out for go ahead and line 'em up. Shoot 'em down like dogs if you want a flock of federal marshals trampin' around here!"

That shocked them into a startled quiet for a moment and he said with his bitter hatred of injustice: "I've been tryin' to get these people out peaceably. Journigan's the guts of this whole farmin' movement; these folks'll start pullin' out when they see the feller that fetched them here locked up in that jail by the man they just got through putting in office. They'll know then they're up against a rigged deal, and they won't risk starvin' their families to prove it. I think —"

Another outbreak of shouting drowned his voice like an avalanche and the end of Pell's gavel snapped and flew across three tables. He flung the handle away and pounded the board with his sixshooter. He glowered at Mark, not liking that crack about a rigged deal, and demanded of him, furious, "You got any more remarks like that you feel you got to get off your chest?"

"I've got a couple, yes. These boys don't seem to understand that what they're up to will cut both ways. Minute you fools grab a gun and resort to violence you're not only invitin' retaliation, you're making yourself a target for every down-at-heels crook in the country. You're sayin', in effect, 'Here it is, boys — come and get it.' And they'll come! Like a plague of locusts! There'll be robbin' and killin' and rapin' and burnin' and, before it's all done with, you'll see U.S. Marshals cuttin' up what's left. If that's what

164

you're wantin', go ahead and start your range war."

The truth in Mark's words hit that crowd like a thunderbolt. More than one tough cowman blanched as men uneasily peered at one another. A lot of questioning stares began to focus on Pell who suddenly looked a little trapped. The Terrapin boss, and more than just a few others, stared at Mark as though only now for the first time seeing him.

"And that's just brushin' the high spots," he told them. "You try movin' these people out forcibly and every owner in this room will be stripped to his water and those that ain't dead will probably land in the pen. Is that what you're wantin' to take these boys into, Pell?"

Pell stared slack-jawed and confounded.

Curly, saturnine eyes surveying this confusion with an open contempt, drawled scornfully, "The man can certainly tell it creepy. What does he use — a crystal ball? Or just the slick gift of gab that's put a credulous old man on the road to the poorhouse?"

Mark, with tight-squeezed lips, saw Pell getting hold of himself and sensed, without being able to stop or deflect it, the insidious poison behind Curly's words. He could guess what Curly was up to but he was tied hand and foot; shackled not only by his rock-hard allegiance and vast loyalty to Muleshoe, but by the immeasurable depths of his debt to Muleshoe's owner. Everything Mark had and was he owed to Curly's father. He could not strike back at Curly without also bringing down Eph Thorpe. And Curly's malicious grin told Mark Eph's son was suddenly aware of this.

"What's this?" Pell asked through the general surprise which had pulled all eyes away from Mark. "Did you say Eph Thorpe's on the —"

"I'll not call Mark Dawson a crook," Curly said, "but on the face of the record he has certainly been a fool. That's putting it in the most kindly fashion I am able to. The buyer who contracted our beef crop told me Dawson insisted we'd take nothing but cash. Then he goes off to that nesters' hoedown at the schoolhouse and, because he gets too preoccupied with chasing some nester's woman through the brush, I am forced to take payment for that beef myself. And was robbed of every cent of it at gun point within the hour. I'm not saying he had anything to do with that stickup. But the very next day we lost seventy head of cattle under circumstances which compelled me to make an investigation."

Suspicion lay bright in the glances men threw at Mark now.

"Consider the record," Curly said, as with extreme reluctance. "My father took young Dawson in after Apaches killed his people in a wagon train massacre. It made no difference that Dad knew nothing about his parents. I was raised with Mark; I ought to know him. Yet I was surprised at the depth of his resentment and bitterness when Dad couldn't afford to send us both off to college. I could see, during my vacations, the ugly thoughts that were working in him, the secret craving for liquor he had let get hold of him, the way he'd slip away of nights to be with women or rough characters my father wouldn't have stood for —"

"And you kept your mouth shut?" Pell cried incredulously.

"Of course. Since that fall off the cliff my father has aged beyond his years. I won't say he's become childish but you should know that, badly as the place has been mismanaged during my absence, Dad in a faith bred of trust and affection will hear no word against him."

"But you could show —"

"And break Eph's heart? You haven't watched him sitting there day after day, trembling hands gripped to the crook of that cane, knowing he faces the same ruin that's threatening all of us yet able gently to smile, secure in the belief Mark will some way pull him out of this. You think I could tell him this wagon train stray, this snake he's taken into his house, has repaid all his kindness with calculated treachery? That this man he has loved like a son has been conniving with squatters —"

"Liar!" Mark's twisted cheeks were taut with outrage.

Curly smiled at him sadly, waving back the four or five men who had got out of their chairs to close in on him. "I wish to God you were right!" A sigh came out of him and he said, "If you're not hand in glove with this riffraff you can show your good faith by moving Rube Krieger off Jugwagon's range. Will you do that?"

"No!"

"Then you're wasting your breath, Mark. I've got hold of the nester who ran off those seventy head you thought had 'strayed'. Baiden, fetch in that man Lefty Red's been holding out there."

The sergeant-at-arms wheeled away. The others eyed Mark through a rising rumble of low-voiced talk. Sick with shock Mark stared back at this crowd unbelievingly.

168

Baiden returned prodding Gunter ahead of him and then took up his place with broad shoulders, like an anchor, set against the glass doors.

"Now," Curly said reassuringly to Gunter, "these men understand you're to be let off light if you make a clean breast of this. Just tell us the truth about those missing Muleshoe cattle."

Gunter's hands appeared a little nervous but his face was composed and his eyes moved about with a glint of amusement that was little short of being downright insulting. Someone growled for Baiden to straighten him out. Pell rapped for quiet and told the fellow to get at it.

With a fine show of insolence Journigan's understrapper told them, "While you lords of creation have been high-bootin' it around shootin' off your yaps about us poor starvin' farmers, one galoot in this room has built up a right smart trade in the beef you boys have been raisin'. Come to me along about three months ago and said if me an' some of my neighbors didn't mind a little ridin' he could put us in the way of makin' a pretty good thing out of it.

"He sure done it, too. After all, we got to eat an' so a few of us throwed in with him, not aimin' to see our kids go hungry while you plutocrats was livin' off the fat of the land. The deal was fifty-fifty — him to tell us where an' when, us to do the actual movin'. I'll say this much for the son of a buck: he knows good stuff when he sees it. And he sure got around enough to see plenty. I'll bet we've got away with five hundred head in the last month alone —"

"All right," Curly said, frowning sternly. "I guess you've given us enough of the general picture. Give us the dope on those seventy-three head of Muleshoes that went off our range the other day in broad daylight."

Gunter grinned. "That was duck soup. I suppose you've heard tell how a coupla weeks back a bunch of Wire Creek Apaches got off the reservation and ripped the Globe stage all to hell an' gone. That stage had the Bell Mine payroll on it. Well, this cow feller had found out where they was holed up an' made a hard-cash deal for seventy-three head to be delivered into them rocks and oak brush north of Fort Grant."

Growls burst out of half a hundred throats and old Hi Gruley, jumping onto his chair, yelled, "Name him! Put a handle on this sidewindin' snake!"

Gunter's cheeks paled a little and some of the cocky look left him when he saw what a tide of passion he'd stirred up; but Curly's voice, riding the wake of Pell's pounding gun butt, cut through the bedlam. "Give them the rest of it first. Tell them how you knew when to come for this stock."

"This feller," Gunter said, "was in town the night before. Said he'd have the stuff ready about ten in the mornin' just south of Muleshoe's east gate. We didn't see him when we got there but there was a big stretch of fence down an' the cattle was bunched in a draw just back of —"

"His name!" Gruley shouted, and half a dozen others swiftly took up the cry.

The nester, half turning, flung out a pointing hand. "It was that feller right there! The Muleshoe ramrod, Dawson!"

Mark felt like a man suddenly kneed in the groin. The staring faces became blurred. The room spun dizzily, went completely out of focus, jerked into clear shape again and unwound, shuddering crazily. His ears were filled with the tumult of shouting. Tables went down like collapsing hurdles as men, surging onto their feet, shoved toward him. Something whined past his cheek and glass crashed behind him and he felt something else cuff the sleeve of his coat. He began to go out of his head a little and Gunter, scared eyes bulging, commenced to back away.

Mark jumped for him, ripping Curly's gun from its holster. He didn't know what he meant to do except some terrible compulsion made it seem at once imperative that he come to grips with this lying little rat of a man and tear the God's truth out of him.

He had no consciousness of swinging but a gash suddenly opened in Gunter's screaming face and a bright red flow of blood welled out of it and someone caught a hold on Mark's left shoulder and he came half around with the gun still lifted and saw Bill Baiden with his hands flying upward abruptly crumple and pitch inertly to the floor.

Three drilled holes suddenly showed in the glass of the doors and, as he stared at these confused, one whole panel collapsed in shattered fragments. He heard the guns then and, jumping Baiden's outsprawled shape, crashed through the doors, reeling into the lobby.

A white-faced clerk sprang out of his path with a frightened yell and Mark was onto the porch in five strides, vaulting the rail, jerking loose the roan's reins. The horse was going full speed when Mark's rump hit the saddle.

12

Rube Krieger, quitting Muleshoe headquarters on the shortcut for town, felt considerably less than satisfied with himself. He was too angrily conscious of a lurking unease and could not get shut of the notion he'd tipped over some kind of an applecart when, stormily rousing the Old Man out of his sleep, he'd slapped the cause of this trip contemptuously into Eph's lap.

Curly's treatment of Lyla was enough to gravel any man and Rube hadn't put any holds on his tongue. He had aired his views using words any mule skinner would be proud to get a copy of, but there wasn't much pride left in Rube's system now. The crumpled look of that old man when he'd banged out of the house was still riding Rube's thinking with nine-point rowels.

What he'd said to Eph had been the God's own truth, only Eph wasn't the one he had gone out there to throw it at. He'd supposed that damned Curly would have hit straight for home and had been too hacked, upon discovering he hadn't, to keep a rein on his temper.

He wished now he'd held his trap shut. Sight of that currency appeared to have meant more to Eph than Curly's use of it had warranted. Instead of showing understandable anger or a natural shame for what lay back of Curly's action, the added total of those banknotes seemed rather to have confirmed some secret dread Eph had been nursing. Dismay, rather than outrage, was what Rube had caught in that shrinking stare.

He didn't understand all he knew about this business, but one thing he was sure of. Soon as he reached Blossom he was going to hunt out Curly, and he dang well meant to get there just as quick as he was able.

Hardly had the sound of Mark's spurred bootheels quit the courthouse than Journigan was at the door of his cell, hammering the gleaming steel and yelling blasphemously for Fraesfield.

"Don't take your temper out on *me*," the sheriff told him. "You think he had that hand in his pocket to keep the wind off his dew-claws? I may be dumb but I sure ain't crazy! All the time he was swearin' out that warrant an' taggin' along to make sure I served it, he had a gun on my bowels an' would've liked nothin' better than —"

"I ain't worryin' about your bowels! I'm scared what them damn weedbenders'll do when they find out Dawson made you —"

"They've already found that out, never fear."

"Are you changin' your tune?" Journigan's eyes were malignant.

"I ain't changin' nothin', and I ain't lettin' you out until I git a order for it."

"You go round to the judge's an' he'll give you a order. He'll get out a writ —"

"I dunno," Fraesfield said. "I'll have to think about that." He stuffed some twist in his mouth. "Luck don't seem to be smilin' your way lately. You had a hatful of notions but they ain't hatchin' good —"

"You're packin' that star, ain't you?"

"Figure to keep right on, too."

"Now listen here —"

"Mebbe it's time I quit listenin'. You sicked that gun fighter on him an' what happened? The gun fighter's finished an' you ain't far from it." The sheriff pushed back his hat and took an impartial view of him. "You don't look near as tough as what you looked a couple days ago."

Journigan took the hide off his language but when he got done Fraesfield's face hadn't changed much. "Nope," he said, thoughtfully, "you don't look near as rugged now you're shut of that gun fighter. Mebbe you better stay a spell an' git rested up."

Mark wasn't thinking when he leaped onto the roan and took off in such a hurry from the front of the hotel. His thought processes, slugged and pounded so unmercifully, were still trying to grasp the whys and wherefores of what had happened; escape and flight had been instinctive, physical phenomena of the strongest urge God gives to man. The same need for self preservation which had caused him to aim his horse toward the border. But before the roan had reached the bluffs above the creek, which a half mile south of town was frequently mistaken for the river it emptied into, his mind began to shake free of its shock induced paralysis.

Bitterly, too late, he saw the full extent of his folly. He couldn't understand how a man could be so stupid. He'd had Eph's son on the defensive, practically whittled down to size, and crazily thrown it all away. Those hours of grace he'd foolishly given him had let the man get his back up, and now

176

Curly'd turned the tables.

An exposed rustler in this country had no alternative but flight.

He remembered Lyla's note and almost groaned aloud in his anguish. He made no effort to curb the roan's headlong pace.

Not until they'd nearly reached the drop going into the water did he swerve the horse enough to make the gouged-out place in the twelve-foot shoulders which passed a wagon road over the unrailed plank bridge that gave the town a crossing.

Not once did Mark look behind him, so certain was his conviction of immediate pursuit. Not until the cut had dropped him below view of the open terrain behind did he slow the pound of those hoofs by a fraction.

His mind was working like lightning now. It had scanned all the angles and summed up his chances and shown him the only course he could follow. As long as it had been at all practical he had done his best to save old Eph from the shock and disillusion of learning the truth about Curly. That much he owed him — and probably more; but he owed something too to the woman he loved, and the lines of that note showed her need was urgent.

He'd no time to delve into what lay back

of her summons; all his energies now were directed toward reaching her. The streambed, bending westward in its sandstone channel, was at this point barely throwrope wide. No growth obscured the nearer shingle but great willows and ancient cottonwoods grayly lined the farther bank. Almost bare at this season of their turned-yellow leaves they yet served to screen the contours of whatever lay beyond them.

A quarter mile downstream the bluffs, through which Mark even now was pounding, sloped away to rolling grassland darkly banded by a stand of oakbrush which for so long as he could remember had been the source of Blossom's firewood.

Mark knew this region thoroughly as he knew Eph's Muleshoe pastures; and sent the roan's flying hoofs clattering over the rattling planks, hearing the hollow reverberations which came booming up off the creek's gray-brown surface. This he knew from experience would be heard back in town. Just short of dirt he jumped the horse into water after lashing Curly's pistol to the horn of his saddle. He slid off the roan's rump and the horse started swimming with him hanging to its tail, doing all he could to turn it toward the shore that was nearest town.

The current, strong in this narrow channel, carried them rapidly westward. They were around the bend, well beyond where the bluffs leveled off, when the roan touched bottom and Mark climbed dripping and shivering up onto the stone-laced sand of the bank. The horse shook itself while Mark dumped water from boots and holster. Curly's beltload of cartridges were probably ruined but he reckoned the five in the gun were still useful. He got it off his saddle, thrust it back in the soggy leather. He heard the bridge boom again beneath fast-traveling horses. Teeth chattering and shaking he waited another full minute before climbing into his stirrups.

The icy grasp of the wind did not go into him so deep once they'd got into the comparative shelter of the brush. His shaking hands were blue with cold and he was thankful Lyla's shack was no farther than it was.

Steam curled weirdly from the coat of his horse and made a kind of churning froth about his own soaked clothing. Although whisked away and almost instantly dissipated it continued to boil off them not as breath on a frosty morning but rather, in this forlorn day, like gray stringers of smoke. Chilled to the marrow Mark was finally forced to stop and get down and pull his clothes off.

He squeezed what water he was able to out of them and rubbed his shivering body with handfuls of dried grass before he got back into them. With teeth still chattering he strapped Curly's shell belt round him and picked up his sopping coat. It was while he was trying to wring the thing out that he discovered Howlett's pistol was still in one of the pockets.

He tossed it into the brush but, after he'd got the coat on again, he scowled and retrieved it. He didn't know why he'd keep a gun that had been wet bad as this one but he returned it to the pocket and, with boots once again thrust into the oxbows, kneed the roan into movement.

This brush stretched unbroken to the west edge of Blossom where the unlocated nesters had their ragtag of tents and flimsy tarpaper shanties. It was this same stand of growth that thinned out around Lyla's and, as he came nearer, some residue of caution made him again forsake the saddle.

He stood shivering awhile, trying to make up his mind. He could not see her place yet because of intervening branches but he could glimpse a back corner of one of its neighbors and guess near enough which direction to move in.

He wasn't worried about finding it. He was being prodded by a feeling Lyla's place might turn out to have been better kept away from. This was what had stopped him, what had brought him down off the horse again.

The roan wasn't showing any sign of alarm.

Even if anyone had happened to recall seeing him earlier headed in this direction with the girl, common sense assured Mark they could hardly expect him to be around here now. Not with that bunch of horse-backers after him. Those were the boys he would have to watch out for.

By this time, no doubt, they'd have discovered he had tricked them. They'd be hunting for his tracks, and when they couldn't find them they'd come back to that bridge. He didn't think they'd manage to cut his sign there either, but they might guess what he had done. They'd probably search both banks in any event and, sooner or later, they'd find where he'd come out. Then, if any of them had seen him with Lyla, they would guess that her shack would be the natural place to seek him.

He could probably count on fifteen minutes.

Satisfied now, he led the roan deeper into the thicket and tied it, for the first time noticing his rifle was gone from the saddle. This brought the drift of his mind back to Curly, recalling the man's penchant for thoroughness. And he remembered Rainey's mention of Curly's forthcoming nuptials, grasping a lot of things now which had before defied understanding.

At first it had been only his plans Eph's son had been protecting — some wild scheme for gain through a consolidation whose success appeared dependent on traveling in double harness with Pell's unattractive daughter. Now, faced with Mark's ill-considered threat of exposure, it was these plus Muleshoe and, he probably imagined, even his life which Curly was fighting for. It was, boiled down, a battle for survival Mark was up against, and that meeting — if it gave no hint of another thing — proved the man would stop at nothing to get Mark out of his way.

The shack looked no different than it had two hours ago. A blue-gray curl of smoke was coming out of the rock-and-mud chimney, downbent and swirled into swift obscurity by the wind that still cried about the shake-covered eaves. The one grimed window that faced him showed the shine of a lamp and this pallid gleam Mark, in his terrible aloneness, found immeasurably comforting.

He swept another look through the gale-bent oaks and across what he could see of those adjacent shacks and, with the clothes stiffening on him, stepped around the corner, moving at once to the door. He had no desire to be seen on the stoop and so, without knocking, straightaway pushed it open, only then remembering he had told Lyla, leaving, to keep the door barred.

He didn't see the gun. He saw Howlett's face and the glint of his teeth, and everything dissolved in a blinding flash of light through which the magnified roar of the gun kept pounding over and over as though it would go on forever.

13

Rube was just about abreast the plank pens of the stockyards when an uproar of angry voices fixed his considering glance on the front of the hotel. With all that racket no one needed to inform him Curly Thorpe and the rest of this country's moguls were in the process of holding another of their meetings. Seemed like every time that bunch got together about all they did was cuss and shout.

He stopped the bay-and-white saddler and sat a spell thinking. What he ought to do, he reckoned, was go right along in there and in front of the whole caboodle tell that cocky scissorsbill he could either do the right thing by the girl or get the living hell beat out of him.

It wasn't fear of personal consequences which made Rube Krieger hesitate. He was a forthright man, long accustomed to speaking his mind as he saw it. Trouble was, by Judas, the son of a buck might do it, and when it came right down to cases Rule was a long way from sure that would be like to pleasure anyone.

He was reaching for the makings, still frowning, still not certain, when an explosion of belt guns scattered his thoughts like quail. He heard glass crash. A bent-double shape appeared on the porch, jumped the rail without pausing and wrapped one stretched hand about the horn of a saddle.

With a startled oath Rube recognized Mark as the Muleshoe ramrod, slogging boot into stirrup, let the wheel of the horse jerk him onto its back. He caught the flash of Mark's gut hooks and, through lifting dust, saw the horse streak off hellbent for the border.

He was still staring after them, baffled and half minded to head that way himself, when men began erupting from the doors of the hotel like ants piling out of a burning log. "There he goes!" yowled one of them, and the whole bunch dived for the broncs tied in front of it.

Rube didn't know whether to go or stay but, after a couple of hard stares at the shapes of those mounting, he decided to hang and rattle. Curly wasn't with them. Pell wasn't, either. None but the hotheads were bouncing into their saddles. He didn't reckon they'd catch anything larger than a cold — not with Mark mounted on a son of Lock's Rondo.

Right now it was Curly that most of Rube's interest was centered in.

He eased his horse back around a corner of the stockyards and, sliding off, reins over arm, hunkered down on his boot-heels where the wind wasn't quite so ferocious, prepared to wait out Curly's appearance. If he could stick to his tail till he got off someplace alone, Eph Thorpe's too-handsome son could have the hell whaled out of him and made to understand he could look for more of the same every time he put a foot across that Lyla girl's doorstep.

Rube reckoned that ought to hold him.

Mark couldn't figure what ailed his vision. He could see, right enough, but everything looked so cockeyed and crazy. Take that door, for instance — where the devil was the bottom of it? And where had Howlett gone?

Beyond the top half of that open door about all he could make out was a wedge of shadowed rafters. Then, glance widening, he saw the whole damn front of the shack, from window level past the slant of the roof, even to the dark wrack of clouds stretched above it.

It was the sky that jarred him, that gave him his first grim glimpse of reality. To see that much sky he had to be outside and he had no recollection of coming out. He'd pushed the door open, stepped in and seen Howlett; after that he could recollect nothing, just that great flash of light . . . and, yes! The report of a gun —

He tried to move his right arm and seemed incapable of lifting it. Fright moved the left and found cold ground beneath his fingers. The shock of that jolted him into full consciousness and he got his left elbow under him and saw the bottom of the door with his right leg sprawled in front of it and his left doubled against the cracked gray upright of the step. He saw the blood then.

It was all over the front of him and gave him such a turn he almost passed out again. He didn't know whether he'd better try to move or not. Then bed springs shrieked and he saw something on the floor just inside beyond his leg, and these things between them got his back off the ground in a hurry.

Pain splintered through him but the right hand, which had been caught under him, came free and there was a gun in it — Curly's gun. He got his leg off the threshold and, clamping his jaws, came onto both knees and saw Howlett. Three slugs had torn through him not a hand's breadth apart and the gun Mark was holding had nothing in it but empties.

The bed skreaked again. Mark got up and saw Lyla. She was stretched face down, spreadeagled across it, tied hand and foot to the posts at its corners. And there was a gag in her mouth.

Mark's legs were inclined to wabble but he got to the cupboard and found a knife. He cut the gag and one of the girl's swollen wrists loose. He guessed, after that, he must again have passed out because the next thing he knew she had his coat and shirt off and was wringing a rag out into a basin. The rag was hot and so was the water and it felt like she had put salt in it.

She moved away a little then and got a square of white cloth she must have ripped from a sheet. He was on his right side and watched her make a neat pad of this. She pressed it folded against the ribs just below his left armpit and told him to hold it there. She went off with the knife toward the foot of the bed, pulled out and threw back the covers. He heard the blade being ripped through the blue-and-buff tick and then she was back with a handful of batting.

"All right, let go." She pressed the batting against him and put the pad over it. "If you can manage to sit up I'll make a better job of it."

He sat up. The room dived precariously as though he and it rode opposite ends of a seesaw. Pain hit him then like the bite of hot iron. Lyla studied him, watching him anxiously. "I'll be all right now — get it wrapped," he grumbled. "How long was I out?"

"Around three minutes that first time; a little longer just now. I feel mighty meechin', gettin' you shot up like this. That varmint taken me off my guard while I was puzzlin' out what you wrote in that note."

"I didn't write any note. We been a couple of chumps. How long have I been here?"

"Might be as long as ten minutes. How you mean we been chumps?" she asked, fetching around the two ends of the bandage and tying them snugly a bit left of center.

"Curly fixed us both notes and we fell for it. Hand me that shirt —"

"You can't put on that wet thing. Anyway, it's all blood. You get under them covers —"

"I got no time to play sick," Mark growled, standing up. He reached for the shirt where it lay on a chair back, and had to reach twice because the room spun around so. He thrust his arms into the sleeves. "You got any forty-five cartridges?"

"Muleshoe, you're not goin' out of this house!"

"I'm goin'," he said grimly. "Don't get in my way." He stuffed the damp tails of the shirt into his pants and put on the coat she had hung by the fire. Then he went over to Howlett. She watched him let himself down to a knee.

She said angrily, "You ain't got the sense you was born with! If you hadn't been reachin' for that hogleg when he fired you'd be strummin' a harp right this minute!"

Mark paid no attention. He was filling a pocket with the loads from Howlett's belt. Now he picked up Howlett's gun; seemed to be listening as he hefted it. She watched while he swapped the used shell for a fresh one. He took Howlett's wet gun out of his pocket and got up, absent-mindedly laying it on the edge of the commode.

"I've got to get out of here."

She thought she understood and said, "You don't need to go on account of the neighbors; they've all cleared out. Lock, stock an' barrel."

Mark brushed it aside. "I wasn't thinking

about them." He removed Curly's gun from its still-soggy carrier, replacing it with the pistol he had got off the floor.

He was refilling Curly's when she said with asperity, "You ain't in no shape to be fiddlin' with them things. Maybe all you got was a couple holes through your hide, but you've lost a mort of —"

"Take care of yourself." Mark grinned at her bleakly. "After I've gone be sure this time you drop that bar into place and don't —" He broke off, scowling, puzzled and not liking it when he saw her, ignoring him, getting into her Mackinaw. "Where you fixing to go?"

"Wherever it is you're goin'." She pawed Rube's pistol out from under her pillow.

"Now, hold on —" Mark began.

"Don't try bossin' *me* around. If you think I'm about to —"

"You're staying right here —"

"I'm doin' nothing of the kind!" She tied a scarf around her hair. Blue it was, and mighty pretty against that copper sheen. "If you're bound to go rammin' around in wet clothes, and so weak a puff of wind'll probably tip you out of the saddle —"

"But damn it," Mark said desperately, "there's a bunch of riled galoots chasin' —"

"They can chase me, too."

He glared in frustration. He knew better than she how weak he was. But he knew also what anger, what intemperate fury, Curly's lies had stirred up in the men who were after him. He could not stand the thought of her faced with such danger. "A bullet," he said sharply, "don't care *what* it goes into."

"If you go, I go."

He tried — between the black gusts of pain ripping through him — to find words to convince her he'd do better alone, but he was talking at a wall. "Time's a-wastin'," she said, and pulled open the door.

They both heard it then; the nearing rumor of shod hoofs growing louder through breaking brush.

Their eyes met and locked.

Mark shoved past her. She ran after him. "You've no horse!" he cried angrily.

"The one that varmint rode must be someplace around —"

"We haven't time to look —"

"Then yours can carry both of us."

He ran on. He reached the roan but she was right at his heels. When he yanked the reins free of the slipknot which held them the sound of the hunters had come unbearably near; so close he could distinguish individual voices.

He caught hold of the stirrup.

"Mark — please!"

He made the mistake of turning his head. Her haunted eyes swept away the last defense he'd raised against this. Without a word he stood aside and, knowing his folly, watched her mount. She gave him the stirrup and he swung up behind.

The roan came to life under the touch of his spurs. Mark had spent a lot of hours in the schooling of this gelding and it offered no objection to the girl's additional weight. Sinew and muscle, in the synchronized beauty of those swift flashing legs, swept them out of the trees on a hard smooth run.

Flecks of white flurried past on the slant of the wind. Lyla's shack dropped behind. They tore into the open across a frozen road and, like a promise of safety, the distant fifty-mile trough of the Aravaipa Valley showed its gale-lashed width between the granite ramparts of Galiuros and Pinalenos. The girl let go of her anchored breath; and in that very moment, as all his life had been, the bitter with the sweet, Mark heard the crack of rifles.

Even in the lee of this stockyards planking the fingers of the wind were beginning to get their nails in him and Rube, after an hour and a half of unrewarded vigilance, was about fed up with waiting. He was standing now so he could stomp his feet but the cold had by this time got into his bones and the lamps of the Alhambra looked to hold more promise than any satisfaction he might get out of Curly.

It lacked a good while till dark, at least a couple more hours, but the overcast sky was so completely leaden lamps were being lighted all over the town. It was sure as hell going to snow before the day was much older, and the way those clouds were piling up it looked like to Rube this range was in for a blizzard — and him with alfalfa still uncut on the ground.

In a way he kind of wished he had stuck to punching cattle. Sure he owned his own place, but where was the good of it? In the eyes of the cow crowd he'd become a thieving nester; and the homesteaders didn't put no trust in him either. They figured, because he had worked for Eph Thorpe and had filed a homestead claim unbothered along the fringe of a cowman's grass, that he had been planted on them and was still in the pay of the barons. And some of them, he reckoned — like that swivel-eyed Gunter, might be nursing some pretty hard feelings for that fool's ride he'd given them the night he'd pulled them off Mark's tail.

And now the cow crowd was after Dawson.

Things had sure got into a hell of a mess.

He had got about there in his turned-sour thinking when he saw Gunter, counting a handful of greenbacks, come out of the hotel and pause on its porch. *What devilment's that skunk been up to?* he wondered, watching the man get into a saddle and turn the bronc's head toward the Stars & Bars. *I thought that twister was working for Journigan.*

He had imagined a short time back to have heard what had sounded like shots in the direction of shantytown. It hadn't bothered him then because he'd been too engrossed with watching for Curly. Now, fed up with this waiting, he got onto his horse and set off toward Lyla's.

His way took him past half a dozen nester's shacks and only one of them showed a light through its windows. All the others seemed to be completely unoccupied and he considered this odd for the time of the day. He cut over to one finally and took a look through a window. Surprised, he got down and pulled open the door. It was empty, all right; nothing left there but rubbish.

In the saddle again he cut across trash-strewn lots to the place with the light in it. "Hey, Frank!" he called quiet like. The lamp went out suddenly.

"What you lookin' for, Krieger?"

Rube, twisting his head, saw the fellow behind him. What bothered him most was the man's glassy stare and the twin gaping bores of the man's sawed-off shotgun.

"Take it easy, Frank. I ain't lookin' for no trouble. All I want to know is what the hell's happened here." He jerked his chin toward the roundabout shanties.

"Pulled out," growled the gun toter. He spat and said, "Yaller-bellies."

"Well, cripes, they didn't just up an' git, did they?"

"You don't see 'em around, do you?"

Rube thought a moment, shook his head. "But, man, what scared 'em?"

"Sheriff picked up Journigan this noon. On Dawson's say-so. Now Dawson's on the run; seems him an' that snake-eyed Gunter's been workin' some kinda deal in stole cattle. Way I got it, the cow crowd's lit a fire under him an' is gettin' things greased for a all-out nester hunt. Lot of these fools has started rollin' their cotton. Now —" he shifted the muzzle of his Greener a little, casually displaying both pulled-back hammers, "if you got all the questions outa your system . . ."

"For God's sake, Frank," Rube cried nervously, "you got to keep that damn thing trained on my middle?"

"I ain't trustin' you no farther'n I could heave a dead cow! If what I hear'n is right, you're the horse's hind end what took the boys up the crick the night that sonofabitchin' tinbadge turned Dawson loose!"

"Ain't you got it through your thick head yet Mark Dawson's the best friend us weedbenders —"

"I'll make damn sure of that if I get him ketched in the sights of this Greener! Go yap that to him now an' keep right on a-ridin'. Because if any of us sees you round here again —"

He broke off, stiffly listening to the sounds of fast travel. These seemed to be rising from the oaks around Lyla's and to be coming, Rube decided, from the hoofs of one horse. Frank's cabin kind of muffled them and was square in the way of Rube's line of vision, but he had no need of sight to imagine what was happening.

A sudden racket of shouting came over the rooftop and was instantly drowned in the crashing of rifles and tumultuous thunder of hard-running horses. This uproar wheeled north and stretched out toward the Aravaipa as Rube and Frank, silent, blackly stared at each other.

"That was Dawson," Rube growled, "an' them cow-prodders after him. Them barons think Mark's been too easy on you boys —"

"They're thinkin' just what I'm thinkin' that he's a bunch-quittin' bastard that would sell his own saddle if it would turn a extry nickel! I hope to Christ they —"

"You don't believe," Rube cried, incredulous, "Mark would never tie up with —"

"I've seen Gunter with the cattle an' that's good enough for me!"

14

Curly, after Fraesfield came in answer to their summons, listened again with Pell and several other ranchers while Gunter brazenly related his story of Mark's duplicity to the sheriff. Fraesfield had him write it down, then administered the oath and had him sign his name to it. Pell and Gruley signed as witnesses.

The sheriff put the document in his pocket and looked at Pell. "You goin' to press this thing?"

"Of course we're going to press it," the Association's president growled. "You know any reason why we shouldn't?"

"Well, I kinda thought . . . him bein' raised up by old Eph an' all —"

"That ain't going to save him. Our members have been losing too much beef lately for anyone to feel lenient toward a man caught stealing from Eph Thorpe who raised the whelp and paid his wages. We're going to push this to the limit."

"Well," Fraesfield said, with a curious look at Curly, "I'll go round up a posse an' get on his trail right away then." He was turning to go when his glance fell on Gunter. "What about this feller?"

"In exchange for the truth," Curly said, "we've offered him amnesty. You're familiar enough with local conditions to understand what Dawson's done against my father and this community would be hard to believe without the testimony of men who've actually been his accomplices. I've no doubt this man, who had charge of the active end of things, will be the prosecution's chief witness."

"I expect that's right, Mr. Thorpe," the sheriff nodded. "I suppose he'll be around . . ."

Curly looked Gunter over bleakly. "I'll see to it that he is."

After the sheriff was gone and Pell with the remaining ranchers had departed to get their horses and saddle up for home, Curly walked through the deserted lobby with Gunter, surreptitiously sliding some folded banknotes into the man's pocket.

Gunter's hand followed the bills and a grin twitched the corners of his saturnine mouth. "You've been pretty white to me, Mr. Thorpe."

With a wink Eph's son told him sternly, "We're counting on you to clinch this case with the jury. See that you hold yourself available."

"You ain't goin' to be disappointed."

Gunter opened the door and Curly strode back across the pine-boarded lobby and asked Tod Jennings for the key to his room. The clerk laid down the hair rope he was working on and got it, after which Curly climbed the skreaking stairs with the expression of one who, faced with a personally disagreeable duty, has acquitted himself in accordance with the precepts of both God and man.

Not until he'd gained the cover of his room did he permit the schooled mask of handsome features to relax and display the satisfaction he'd been forced to hug in secret.

A wild glee churned the dynamic depths of his stare; the reshaping of his lips was not unlike the grin of Gunter. Men were such puking fools, he thought derisively. Success — the shrine of so many — was a pattern, a trend and not a formula.

Now that it lay within his grasp he was amazed he had not discovered this sooner. In its final analysis, success was nothing more than the adroit exploitation of the illusions and cravings of more gullible others. Men made a practice of believing what they wanted to believe; you had only to play on their fears and their fancies and you could lead them around by the nose like stuffed rabbits.

He felt pleased with himself — mighty pleased, and he chuckled. He could laugh at Mark now. He could thumb his nose at him. If he wasn't dead already, via that cabin trap and Howlett, he'd be taken care of speedily. Just as soon as one of these riled cowmen got his shape focused over a barrel.

Gunter was on his way out of the country; the nesters who'd helped him were already gone. Gunter's sworn statement accused Dawson of murder, which took care of Pop Henshaw and any danger from juries. Mark Dawson would never be put on the stand; he'd be shot in the brush if he got clear of Howlett. Neither the cow crowd nor Fraesfield's posse would care to take any chances with a man as ungrateful as that renegade from Muleshoe; they'd shoot first and talk later. Yet, even if Dawson should survive and stand trial, who would ever believe him?

Who would believe the girl, either, for that matter? After that is, White Howlett got through with her. He hadn't told Howlett to do one damn thing. All he'd said was Mark would be there — that Lyla was the girl Mark had had in the cottonwoods. And then he'd casually mentioned his own experience with her.

He took off his sheepskin coat and tossed it onto the bedspread. He got a cigar from the newly-opened box on the bureau and sat down with a comfortable sigh by the window, not bothering to light the lamp. It was snowing out now and pretty soon it would be dark.

He carefully pared the end off his expensive cigar, got it lit and puffed a bit, enjoying its fine aroma. He rocked awhile then in the glow of future prospects. Maybe a little later he'd go downstairs and eat. If no reports had come in about Dawson perhaps he'd drop a hint, or prime someone else to get the thought going, that a talk with Dawson's paramour might possibly throw fresh light on the fellow's whereabouts.

Not that it would, or that she'd be available, but a visit to that shack had ought to bring out what had happened there, whether Mark was dead or Howlett. Unless temper had shaken Howlett's aim, or he'd got careless . . .

Tomorrow, Curly mused, he would marry Pell's long-toothed daughter and then, with

Pell's help, he would start laying pipe to take over this country, to buy or freeze out the smaller spreads round about them. Mark had certainly been right about one thing. With Journigan in jail the back of this homesteader menace was broken; already several families had pulled out and more were packing. With this snow coming on a good six weeks in advance of usual, it wouldn't take much to put the whole bunch on the move.

He found this attractive to contemplate; and then he thought, still scanning the likelihoods, it might be smart to spend the night right here and forget those weedbenders. There was always the chance of carrying a good thing too far. After all, he'd buried his tracks and set in motion the machinery that would insure his ultimate triumph. Mark, if he wasn't already past meddling, would hardly have a chance to get in touch with Eph now. A smart man, Curly decided, ought to know when to let well enough alone.

He showed the edge of a smile and settled back in his rocker, finally resolved to let events run their course. He was twisting to flick the ash off his costly cigar when plodding hoofs and a lift of wagon sound drew his glance to the street below.

An old man in a buckboard with a robe over his knees.

Curly's stare abruptly widened. Astounded, he got up and put his nose against the window. He grabbed the sheepskin coat off the bed and shrugged into it.

By the time he got to the lobby his face, though pale, was composed and unreadable. The clerk saw nothing unusual in his appearance. Offering customary lip service he said with a smile, "Aiming to catch a breath of air before you go in to supper?"

The heir to Muleshoe nodded. None would have guessed he was enormously concerned. He even paused to touch a match to his forgotten corona before, fastening his coat, he stepped out into the falling snow.

He saw the wagon at once. Across the frozen ruts of the trafficless street it was stopped, plainly visible, against the lamplighted windows of Lang's Oyster House. Eph, still on the seat, was bent forward, body twisted, as he wrapped the ribbons around the handle of the brake.

With fleeting irrelevance, as he moved through the damp swirl of falling flakes, Curly thought of Pell's daughter and approved his decision to set the date of their wedding a full day ahead. He couldn't imagine what had fetched his father out in this kind of weather over so many miles all by himself in a wagon. It was the first time he'd been to town since his fall and it didn't seem likely he'd have gone to so much effort to get a taste of Lang's cooking.

Now the old man was climbing out of the wagon, a pretty painful process if you could judge by the look of it, but Curly didn't call or hasten forward to help him. Not until his father was away from the windows, moving around the building's corner and, in his string-halt cane-tapping fashion, was obviously bound for the stairs that went up to the second story, did Curly break from his stride, the significance of Eph's destination suddenly driving him forward without regard for appearance.

He lunged onto the walk and was swiftly across it, catching up with the rancher just as Eph reached the stairs. "Dad!"

Eph turned his head and surveyed his son without speaking.

"What in the world are you doing here, Dad?"

"I'm goin' up to see old Struthers."

"I rather fancied you were — but on a day like this! It's not that important, is it?"

"It's important to me."

Curly smiled. "I suppose it is. A man

doesn't visit his lawyer without considerable thought on the subject. What's bothering you?"

"Nothing's bothering me now. I'm going to change my will."

"I'm glad you've got over your illusions about Mark."

Eph looked at him straightly. "I wasn't thinking about Mark."

Neither pair of eyes wavered. "I expect we had better talk this over a little," Curly said, taking hold of his father's arm. "We'll drive around for a spell and you can tell me about it."

"I can tell you right now. I'm leaving Muleshoe to Mark."

"We'll talk it over," Curly said in a tone more appropriate to the discussion of weather. "I think, as your son, I'm entitled to full particulars."

He helped his father back into the wagon, solicitously covered up his legs with the robe. Moving around its whitening bulk then he untwisted the lines and, climbing the wheel, slid into the far half of the snow-dampened seat.

"It's no good," Eph said wearily.

Curly clucked to the horses.

15

"This snow," Mark said, "may help us."

"I don't understand how," Lyla answered. "It's turned wet and it's sticking. They'll follow our tracks —"

"Got to find them first. They haven't found the horse yet; and, if they don't find him soon, by the time they've backtracked to where we slid off there won't be anything to see when they get there."

Mark had known the instant those rifles started banging they would never get clear aboard that overburdened roan. He'd whipped the horse around two shacks and sent it into the trees again. This maneuver had been spotted. The pursuit had changed course, too, but Mark had gained enough slack to put a screen of oak behind them. By the time the cursing riders had reached their place of vanishment the fugitives were out of sight again, and the cowmen had been making so much racket themselves they had no idea which direction the quarry had taken. When they finally realized they were being outfoxed the ground was too cut up with tracks to tell anything.

What Mark actually had done was return to the trail laid down by the hunters when they'd tracked him to Lyla's. But he had got a little too smart.

Giving his pursuers credit for more sense or luck than they had so far shown — and expecting any moment to be again surrounded by the whine and slap of unseen lead — he had abandoned the roan before this had been necessary, thus throwing away the best half of the advantage he might have gained from the pursuit's confusion.

The girl said, "I can hear them," and Mark bitterly nodded.

"Beatin' brush," he grunted, scowling through the snow-induced gloom. It was angering to know that had they still been aboard the horse they might now have gotten clear.

Lyla asked, "Why are they after you?"

So he told her what had happened at the cattlemen's meeting, how he'd been accused of rustling — of stealing even from old Eph, the man who had befriended him; and of Gunter's substantiation. "Rustlin' from them others would have been enough to hang me, but there's no crime more despised on the range than takin' a man's salt and then doing him dirt."

"But you didn't steal any cattle."

Mark laughed shortly. "No one else will ever believe that. There are too many other things involved in this business. A Muleshoe rider has been shot in the back. We lost the money from our beef crop and a —"

"But the part that's really got their goats depends on the word of this fork-tongued Gunter?"

"Well, it does and it doesn't," Mark said, considering. "Most of the suspicion seems to have been stirred up by Curly. Been resentment among some of the cow bosses, too, over me bein' picked to deal with these homesteaders. A lot of folks think I've been too easy on them fellers."

He explained his convictions. "The whole thing's a mess but you can't really pile all the blame on these farmers. They got a right to live too, and they come here in good faith —"

"You're not answerin' my question."

"I'm tryin' to. What's happened to me ain't so much because of what Gunter said as because it tied in with things they've been conditioned to suspect through other sources. Talk has got around that except for my carelessness — occasioned," he said gruffly, "by an 'unhealthy' interest in nesters — Muleshoe wouldn't have lost the money it got for its beef crop. Other talk suggests I might have been mixed up with the men who stole that money. Curly's talk at the meetin' gave suspicion a lot of weight. Gunter's talk was the final straw."

They moved awhile without speech then, occasionally forced to crouch almost double as they crossed little snow-mantled patches of open. And hatefully the sound of the pursuit's noisy progress, like an unwanted hound, tagged steadily, almost inexorably, after them.

Mark cautioned the girl. "Don't disturb these branches any more than you have to. Some of that bunch might miss the snow we knock off them. It'll still be noticeable after our tracks —"

Lyla interrupted him. "Why does Curly hate you?"

He glanced at her and wheeled his eyes to the front again. "I don't know. I used to figure we was pretty good friends but things have been a lot different since he got back from school. We ain't seen too much of —"

"What was that you was sayin' about Muleshoe losin' some money?"

Mark recounted the story Curly'd told

him and Eph. He mentioned visiting the buyer and what the man had said about Curly insisting on being paid in cash.

Lyla stared at him, startled.

"You mean foldin' money? He gave me quite a chunk of foldin' money the other night."

Mark's head came around. "Curly gave *you* money?"

"More than five thousand dollars," she told his rummaging eyes.

"But why would he do a crazy thing like that?"

Color swept through her cheeks and then her chin came up and she let him know angrily, "That's sure a fool question! Ain't you heard it told yet he's aimin' to travel in double harness with some Big Mogul's daughter?"

"What's that got to do with it?"

"Honeylamb, you ought to be bored for the simples." She peered up at him slanchways. "Do you reckon she's prettier than I am?"

"I don't get it," Mark growled.

"Don't get what?"

"The connection. Unless —" He looked at her sharply. "You mean he gave you that money to get out of town?"

"I think that was mostly what he had on

212

his mind. He might of figured he owed me a part of it anyway." Her cheeks were tight, scornful, but her glance didn't try to slide away from Mark's face; and, when he continued to stare like it didn't make sense to him, she said without pride or defiance but not apologizing either, "We got pretty thick while he was goin' to school in Texas. I was biscuit shootin' in that town and he was carryin' me around right considerable towards the last."

Mark felt sick, her face drifted away from him. Something seemed to be vibrating inside his head. And then his vision cleared. Her face swam back into focus and he said, coldly furious: "What became of the money?"

She looked angry, too. "I pitched it out in the road!"

Mark realized he was shaking. He was burning up and freezing and all the blood he had left seemed to be hammering through his brains. When at last its roar subsided the racket of the riders was unconscionably louder, dangerously near them; and he caught hold of her arm. "We've got to get out of here."

She jerked her arm away from him. "You won't be needin' me . . ."

"Don't be a fool — of course I need you!"

"I saw the way you looked just then. You wouldn't have any use for a whore —"

"Don't talk like that!" He said gruffly, "There's a hell of a lot of difference between a whore and what you've done —"

"You don't have to whitewash me, Mark Dawson! He never took nothin' I wasn't proud an' willin' —"

"You made an honest mistake. This world would be a pretty sorry damn place if —"

"I saw your face!"

"I was thinkin' of Curly." He caught her arm again and broke into a run, but she continued to hold back. There was a wistful look mixed with the strain in her expression but she was too essentially honest, a great deal too much in love with him to risk a glimpsed future not founded on full truth.

"You ain't heard the whole of it. I was wild when he come to my place with that money. I was goin' to make him sorry if it was the last thing I did. I was —"

"I know," Mark said. "You made up your mind that you was goin' to have Muleshoe. Probably in your place I'd of felt the same way; but you're not doin' it, Lyla. You're — *Quick!*" he growled hoarsely.

Regardless of thorns — and this damned brush was full of them — he pulled her into the cover of a thicket of chaparral. And barely in time.

Less than twenty feet away three glowering riders crashed into the open and, staring around, pulled up for a breather. "You'd think, in this snow, we woulda caught 'em by now," the tallest one said, blowing on his cold fingers. And the shortest man grunted, "It's a bitch of a day t' have t' spend chasin' round through this goddam brush."

The third rider didn't say anything. He sat with a knee over the horn of his saddle and kept peering off through the snow-laden branches. The tall man said, "Well, we better git at it," and the short one groaned. "I'm s' damn wet now I might just as well've been holdin' Maud's youngest. Where you reckon that sonofagun's got to?"

The third rider said through a mouthful of twist, "I can tell you one thing; he sure ain't headed for Muleshoe. And he ain't far off, either, ridin' double like he's doin'. I think what we oughta do is work through to the east of this brush —"

"You don't think," the tall one said, "that buck's goin' to head for town, do you?"

The tobacco chewer nodded. "Stands to reason. You'd see it if you tried usin' your head instead of your elbow. He's played out on this range. His best bet's the border.

He's got to get another bronc or ditch the girl, an' he knows it. So he'll try to get over near as he can to the town. It's almost dark now. He'll wait a quarter hour, mebbe, an' try to slip the girl in where she can —"

A muffled shout cut through his words, immediately followed by three gunshots. All three stood up in their stirrups, listening; then the tall and the short one scratched with their steel and went slashing through the oaks in the direction of the racket. The third rider spat and, following his own convictions, moved his paint pony off at a walk, heading east.

Mark waited three minutes, cautioning the girl to silence. Then he helped her out of the brush, feeling weak as a kitten. Lyla said, "Their horses was standing right on our tracks." She looked at him worriedly. "You better take it easy —"

"I'll make out. They've found the horse. They'll know we're not far away now. Come on," he muttered, and struck off toward the south.

"What was you about to say when them fellers butted into our talkin'?"

"We'll try to reach the river. We'd never get into town from the east now. Squidge will be watchin' —"

"You said I wasn't goin' to try for

216

Muleshoe. You said, 'You're —' and then those fellers come along. Go on, tell me the rest of it. Why won't I try for Muleshoe?"

"Because, if we get out of this, you're goin' to marry me."

Rube was back at his post by the corner of the stockyards, remembering the sight of Gunter quitting the hotel counting those greenbacks, when he heard the team wheel into the street. It was commencing to snow in grim earnest. The light wasn't good and he had to stare into the teeth of the wind, but he had worked for Eph Thorpe far too long not to know him when he saw him go past on the seat of a wagon.

Rube looked after him, astonished. He'd understood the old man was confined to the house. He had certain sure looked to be on his last gasp when Rube had gone out there and, not finding Curly, had dumped that bundle of banknotes in his lap. He had sure looked bad, Rube remembered.

He kicked his numbed feet against an upright, hoping to knock a little warmth into them, and tried to think what purpose could have seemed sufficiently urgent to have fetched that old man into town in this weather. He saw the horses pulled to a stop before the Oyster House up yonder and, with an abrupt and quickening interest, saw Curly come out of the hotel and start toward Muleshoe's wagon.

He watched the old man get down and turn away from the windows; saw Curly, breaking into a run, catch his dad at the foot of those outside stairs that went up the gray flank of the building to the office of Lawyer Struthers. Then the pair, with Curly gripping Eph's arm, turned around and went back and got into the wagon.

"Well!" Rube said, pleased, and climbed into his saddle.

The pursuit, dimmed by distance, was an erratic pulse of indeterminate sound behind the still-falling flakes when Mark and the girl, raggedly panting, came out of the woods into the snow-blanketed grass below the bend of the creek.

Mark, though he had managed thus far to hide it from Lyla, was reeling with weariness. Fighting that brush had taken a lot of the sap out of him and it was a cinch he was going to have to get some rest soon.

The wind had fallen but his face was too hot to feel natural in this weather and his bullet-torn side ached like an ulcerated tooth. But he was still clear-headed and gave God thanks for it.

It was full dark now — as dark as it would get in this snow. Not dark enough to give a man much protection if he were forced to hide again. The slope stretched white and unbroken to the blackness of the water, which was bad, for it had been his plan to work east along the shore behind those bluffs till they reached the wagon road.

Lyla looked at him anxiously. "Are you all right, Muleshoe?"

"I was thinkin'," Mark said. Alone he would have taken his chances but with Squidge on the prowl someplace to the east of them he hated to risk crossing that broad band of white. But there was nothing else for it. The brush was full of riders who were steadily working closer. Why didn't the fools give up and go home?

She put a hand on his arm. "What are you trying to do?"

"We've got to get back to town. That's the only place we can get horses now —"

"You wait here," she said. "I'll find horses for us."

He considered. "No —"

"But they're not huntin' *me*."

"We don't know what they're doing."

"But you can't afford to be seen in town. They think you're the one who's been back of all that rustlin' —"

"I haven't forgot. If I could just get my hands on Gunter . . ."

"How can you? How will you find him?"

That was the rub. No matter what arrangements the man had made — or had made for him — he would surely not be fool enough to remain where he could be got at. He had obviously been well paid for his lies and, with the money in his pocket, was probably well on his way to getting out of the country.

Everywhere he turned Mark banged his head against a wall.

He was no more anxious to die than the next man, nor did he wish to spend the rest of his existence dodging posses, as he knew he would have to if he quit this town now. He wanted for himself a useful life built on tasks and problems with which he was familiar — a life shared by Lyla and respected by his neighbors. But he was practical enough to realize this was impossible without he could clear his name.

And there was another rub.

As things stood now, to clear himself he must make Gunter confess the truth, and the truth was a bony finger pointing arrow-straight at Curly.

Well, and what if it did? He wasn't Curly's keeper. He had done all he could to keep the man out of trouble. Whatever came of the truth Curly — by his insatiable greed for power, by his own acts and ruthless scheming — had invited anything which might happen. Mark could tell himself this was just and equitable, but it was only one side of the picture. On the other side was Eph, the man to whom Mark owed everything.

He must have groaned aloud, for Lyla took hold of him. He shook off the touch of her, scrubbing a hand across his unshaven cheeks. "I'm all right." But he wasn't and guessed he never would be again.

He'd have to let Gunter go. Loyalty and honor weren't just a couple of words a man could toss aside when it suited him. He owed Lyla something too, and himself, he guessed likely; but Eph came first. He'd worked hard all his life and was an old man now. An old man facing the future on the crutch of his faith in Curly.

Mark reckoned he never would forget this day but he saw his way now, understood what he had to do. He had stalled long enough. It was time to start running.

16

It took the better part of a two-hour ride to get from Gunter's place on Ten Mile Creek and, having correctly interpreted the wink he'd been given along with Thorpe's instructions to hold himself available, Gunter was inclined to waste no time in digging for the tules. That cow crowd right now was a mighty riled bunch. Should anything go haywire with their plans for hanging Dawson they might very well decide to stretch a nester in his stead.

Also there was Dawson.

Gunter's mind shied away from the thought of what might happen if Muleshoe's ramrod ever caught up with him. He'd persuaded himself there was no likelihood of that, but a man never knew what the next hour might hold for him. Look at Journigan! Fraesfield had quit him like a cold potato after Dawson had dumped that stiff in his lap.

He flung off his lathered horse and, catching up a rope, ducked into the pole corral and looped him out a fresh one, a linebacked dun that was fast and enduring as any bronc he owned.

He pulled the gear off the horse he'd come in on, slapped the sweat-soaked blanket and saddle on the rolling-eyed dun, kicking him in the belly when the animal tried to swell up. He jerked the cinch tight and tied the reins to a chinaberry just outside the door. Then he went into the shack to dig up his buried plunder.

He had made quite a haul off his eight weeks of rustling. His coat pockets were bulging when he finally stood up. He sure hated to think he had come to the end of it, but he was smart enough to know that, with the steals pinned on Dawson, Thorpe would tolerate no more.

He gnawed a piece of cold meat while he considered where he'd head for. Mexico was closest, but if Dawson got clear of the bunch that was after him that was the place he'd be making tracks for; and Gunter sure didn't want to see no more of that jasper.

Damn! He sure hated to go off and leave this fine bottom land. Easily the best quarter section in the whole goddam country! And all those horses he'd glommed onto! And the backlands fair crawling with summer-fattened cattle. . . .

He went completely still, even his jaws ceasing to function as he stared with narrowed eyes at the board he'd pulled out of the floor. Cattle . . . By God! He'd be a fool to yank up his picket pin now. Curly wasn't the only one who could make a good thing out of cattle! He had a gold mine in Curly if he played this right.

He cut another slab of meat for himself and, swinging one leg with his hip on the table, carefully scanned the possibilities and, satisfied, got up. Curly would be wild but what the hell could he do?

Though he dreaded the chore he was faced with now, Mark knew by the tension building inside him it would only grow worse the longer it was put off. Someway he'd got to tell Lyla, and he felt lowdown enough to eat from the same plate with Curly.

He let go of his breath and said, "We better get movin'." He could feel her eyes boring into him worriedly as they worked slowly creekward through the cushioning carpet of snow-clogged grass. They were like sitting ducks against this unbroken whiteness and he suddenly realized the flakes had quit falling.

Horse sound and breaking brush, grown stronger in the branch-blurred blackness behind them, continued to reveal the persisting presence of riders. Judging by cadence there were not as many of them now; but these would be the die-hards, that grimly earnest more dependable element, the just and the righteous who wouldn't take less than his life for their losses.

Though he wasn't cold Mark shivered.

A little foretaste, he thought bitterly, of what it would be like all the rest of his days, hunted and hounded from pillar to post, knowing every man's hand was against him. But it stiffened his resolve.

When the stream was a broad band of murmurous darkness forty yards in front of them, he said, "I can't take you, Lyla."

"Can't take me where?"

"Into the hell I'm probably bound for."

"Are you going to start that all over again? We settled that once. Where you go, I go."

"Not any longer." He felt the sharpness of her glance but kept his own fixed on the water. This was harder than he had reckoned but it was something he had to do. "I was out of my head if I spoke to you of marryin'."

They took several steps in silence. Mark's

whole self cried out against this. Every sinew of him fought it but he kept his jaws clamped tightly, kept his bleak glance straight ahead. Then her voice came out of the crunch of their bootsteps, low and sweetly wistful; a knife turning in him. "I ain't askin' you for marriage. When a girl feels toward a man the way I feel about you —"

"No!" Mark almost shouted it. Mouth awry, he said harshly, "Whatever was between us, it's over now and done with. Done with — do you hear me?"

"My heart says you're lyin', Muleshoe. It's in your mind somethin' bad is goin' to happen. You're tryin' to prot—"

Huskily, Mark Dawson swore.

"Hardship's all I've ever known. I can get along without brass lamps —"

"I've got to *run!* Can't you understand that? What kind of a dog do you think I am to be draggin' a woman through a life of —"

Her hand came up and stopped his lips with her fingers. "A good kind, Mark . . . and you won't have to drag me; I would go to the ends of the earth with you — *gladly.* Do what you have to do, only . . . don't ever leave me."

With a sound of despair, he pulled her into his arms.

★ ★ ★

Rube hadn't the faintest notion of where Curly and Eph were bound in that wagon; the why and the where of the matter never touched him. He followed only in the hope this trip might take Curly where a middling spry man could work him over sufficient that his future appearance would not ensnare gullible females. Rube's fists sorely ached to get at Curly's face.

He was surprised when the man turned south toward the creek. He could not think what business would be taking them that way. He did not let it bother him though; he hadn't any intention of trailing them much longer. All he wanted was to get that polecat far enough from town that his howls wouldn't put too quick an end to this shindy.

With disconcerting abruptness the big flakes quit falling. It was dark now, full dark, but the glistening mantle of white over everything improved visibility enormously. The wagon stood out sharp against the snow and Rube discovered it had stopped. It was hardly seventy feet from him, but so engrossed in their discussion were the pair on its seat neither one of them thought to look behind.

The old man was taking something out of

his pocket — kind of looked like them banknotes Lyla'd pitched from her shanty. Eph was talking and you could see Curly wasn't much liking the sound of it. He growled something sharp in a quick protesting voice, but the old man shook his head. "You've had all the chance you're goin' to get."

Curly jumped to his feet. Rube saw his arm lash out; saw the old man, struck, fall into the bed of the wagon.

Rube stared, mouth agape. Then, swearing, sent his mount plunging forward, not caring whether Curly saw him coming or not.

Possibly he did; more likely he didn't. He stayed crouched there a moment with one hand in the seat. Thrusting something inside his sheepskin coat, he whirled, caught up the lines and, wheeling the horses off at an angle, snatched up the whip and brought it down in a whistling arc. Again and again he struck them until the crazed team was bolting in a paroxysm of terror.

Crouched above them, hat gone and hair flying, Curly looked like a madman wielding that whip. Nothing could withstand the wicked fury of such punishment.

Rube used his spurs in appalled desperation but his bronc hadn't the breeding that was back of Eph's horses and they continued to gain, panicked now beyond stopping. Knowing only the need to get away from the flail that was slicing the back halves of their hides into ribbons, they were bound like a tidal wave straight for the bluffs.

A hoarse sob skreaked out of Rube. He shouted and cursed at them. He saw Curly jump, saw his shape hit and bounce and roll in a tangle of arms and legs outflung grotesquely. He didn't catch the glint of metal, didn't see the streak of flame that spurted out of the sheepskin coat. All he knew was that something hit him, driving the air from his lungs like the hoofs of a mule. The world stood on end and turned black and exploded.

Gunter, with his loot left behind, rode into Blossom from the west and in that weird half darkness combined of night and snow stopped his linebacked dun beside the planks of the stockyards. He had a long look around before, kneeing his horse through patches of lamplight dappling the street's white-shrouded surface, he cut down a lane to leave his mount at the livery.

Old Man Whintlace wasn't around, which suited Gunter just as well. He took care of the horse himself, rubbing the animal and graining it. By backlots, then, he slipped around to the hotel and, not yet anxious for attention, made his entrance via the kitchen.

Three or four ranchers were sitting glumly in the lobby. These lifted dark scowls at him but no one offered any opinions. The mess Mark had made getting out of the place had been swept up, the broken doors removed from their hinges. Through the arch thus provided several patrons could be seen levering food to their faces about the rearranged tables in the dining room.

Not glimpsing Curly among their number, he went over to the desk and asked the clerk where he could find him.

"Mr. Thorpe isn't here right now. Stepped out a bit ago to catch a lungful of fresh air." The clerk made it plain he didn't rate this fellow much above common dirt. "Care to leave any message?"

Gunter showed his teeth. "I'll jest set around an' wait, bud."

Mark and Lyla, following the shoreline, tramped through the snow in silence, working steadily east toward the unseen bridge. Halfway around the bend of the creek Mark came out of his thinking to growl in frustration, "This is a pile of damn foolishness, Lyla. You know it."

"When did love ever take any advice from common sense?"

"But I told you I'd take you with me. I'm not trying to run away from you. All I'm asking you to do is —"

"Wait here till you get the horses. But what if you don't get them? What if you run into a trap and get shot?"

"We don't have to *both* get shot —"

"There are worse things a woman can face than getting shot, Mark."

"We're doubling the danger if we both go in —"

"All right. You stay here then. *I'll* slip in and pick up the horses."

Mark got his legs into motion again, sensing the futility of further words on the subject. The girl tramped along beside him, also silent, a great deal more worried than she was letting him see.

"What do you reckon will happen here now? I mean between the farm crowd and these big barons like your own boss who have fenced off the land?"

"If the homesteaders holler, federal Marshals will come in. They may send a few down to look around anyway. The days of the open range are done — too many people and not enough land."

"You think the cowmen are licked?"

"They'll have to find other ways if they aim to stick with cattle. It may be a good thing. Present methods are outworn. Have to go in more for quality."

"If you were stayin' what would you do?"

"String along with Eph, I reckon."

"If they made him give up the land?"

Mark's side ached too bad to let him put any real thought on it. Face felt hotter, too. He guessed the fever was beginning to take hold of him a little. He wondered how much longer he'd be able to keep going.

"Would you start a place of your own if they took Muleshoe away from Eph?"

"I guess probably." Mark rasped a hand across his cheeks. "It don't make much difference what I'd do. We ain't goin' to be —"

He let the rest of it go, freezing into his tracks and forcing the girl to stop, too. Somewhere — and seemingly over their heads — rushed a thunder of hoofs growing louder and wilder against the rattle and bang of a bounding wagon. Through this uproar ripped the din of a shot. The wagon's racket continued and the turmoil of hoofbeats, building rapidly into an avalanche of sound, drummed fullblown into silence.

From this monstrous quiet, wedded vein to vein by the flesh of fear, came the agonized scream of a terrified horse. Shrill and awful it soared. Something struck shore and water with a resounding crash.

Mark was running, shocked and crazy, around the angle of the bend, Lyla hard on his heels, when a babble of voice sound flung him back on the girl. With locked jaws he stood, one arm holding her back, widened eyes on the shapes of milling horsemen up ahead. In a murmurous huddle these were shifting and swaying along the white shore just beyond the plank bridge.

"What is it?" she whispered.

"Can't see. Sounded like a wagon. Must've gone off the bluffs. This ain't no place for us — that's Dink Fraesfield, that gaunt one. We come damn near walkin' right into his posse."

He pulled her back out of sight. The bluffs along here, of lesser stature, were more sloping. Be hard climbing with this snow all over them, but Mark couldn't see that they were left any choice. With riders behind them and riders ahead their only chance to get clear, without they cared to risk swimming, was to climb up out of this as quick as they were able. He grasped her arm. "We've got to hustle. That bunch from the woods'll be down here in a minute."

It was slippery work, and dangerous, but

three minutes later they crawled onto flat ground and saw the lights of town winking and twinkling in the distance. The girl's teeth were chattering in spite of her exertions.

Mark's glance swept the terrain, discovering a riderless horse — or what looked to be one — standing motionless against the dull gleam of the snow some three hundred feet to the right of them.

"Wait here," he said, and moved off, intending to stalk it. But Lyla came running after him and the horse, throwing up its head, whirled and bolted.

Mark choked back his riled groan. They were like to have their work cut out getting into town now from this direction. Any moment a part of that posse might come riding up onto these flats to find out what had caused what had happened to that wagon, and two people on foot would attract instant notice. He didn't think it was dark enough for falling flat to hide them.

Lyla clutched at his arm. "Off there!" she said, her free hand pointing.

Looking that way Mark finally picked up a moving shape against the lights of the town. A man on foot and moving rapidly away from them. But he was too weary, too flushed with fever, to waste thought on a walker who was that far off. "Come on," he grunted, and they struck off at a tangent. But suddenly her fingers tightened again about his arm and, following her look, he saw the dark blotch huddled yonder in the snow. The girl tried to pull him away but Mark veered stubbornly toward it.

It was a man, face down, arms outflung, one leg doubled under him.

Mark pulled him over, seeing the stain in the snow; softly cursing when he saw the man's face. "Rube!" the girl whispered.

Mark dropped down on one knee, running a hand inside Rube's brush jacket. The man was alive and that was all. His face was gray, his eyes wide open; the cloth of his shirt was soaked with blood.

Mark rubbed snow on his face. "Hold his feet up," he muttered. But the frozen stare wouldn't focus. Mark redoubled his efforts without noticeable progress.

"Oh, Mark —" Lyla cried, "he —"

"Be still," Mark growled, and bent to Rube's moving lips.

"Curly — it was Curly," Rube whispered. "Run his . . . old man over . . . cliff in that wagon."

17

Gunter, despite a perfect understanding of his status in this lobby, was entirely unruffled by the scowls he was attracting. Let these cow fools glower if it pleasured them.

He moved across to the window and stood considering the blue-gray street, grinning at the look that would come over Curly's face when he came into this lounge and discovered Gunter's presence. But that would be as nothing to how he'd look when Gunter told him. The smug bastard would squirm like the hooked worm he was; but in the end he'd pay off, and keep right on paying unless he wanted to see his plans knocked higher than a kite.

It was a good kind of feeling Gunter had as he stood by that window. From a despised and shoved-around nester he'd climbed into a position where he could shove some himself — and don't think he wasn't going to enjoy it! That stuck-up son would pay, all right. He would sooner kick in than do his kicking on a rope, which he was smart enough to know he'd probably do if he got nasty.

Gunter noticed the snow had quit falling.

Clinking some coins in his pocket he watched a couple of half-froze riders fade past. Looked like some of that bunch who'd gone out after Dawson.

Then, abruptly, he caught sight of his goldmine.

He had no idea where the man had come from and was too pleased to see him to waste time wondering. He grabbed up his hat and stepped outside.

Curly, mounting the snow-mantled steps, had got almost to the door when he stopped dead in his tracks. "What are *you* doing here?"

Discovering no sign of a shellbelt on him, Gunter let his fist fall away from his hip. "That any way to greet an old friend like me?" A grin twitched his lips. "Kinda reckoned you might be wantin' to hash over old times."

"I thought you were getting out of this country."

"Well, there ain't no great rush. They ain't caught Dawson yet." Gunter looked like the cat about to swallow the canary. "I kinda figured you and me was *buen amigos,* Curly. In your boots I'd be feelin' almighty friendly towards the gent that put the hex on the guy that was fixin' —"

"You been well paid for that."

"What's a couple of hundred to the gent that gets Muleshoe?"

Curly stared at him a moment. "How much do you want?"

"Well, that's more like it," Gunter chuckled. He considered the rancher foxily. "How much you got in your pockets?"

For a moment he thought he might have gone too far. But when he saw Curly shrug he knew he had his fish hooked.

"Around six thousand."

"Guess that'll square it."

"You think I'd be fool enough to hand you a wad of that size on this porch?"

Gunter's lips cracked away from his teeth in a grin. "I sure as hell ain't goin' off noplace with you!"

Curly kept his voice down. "Understand, by God, this is the last chunk you'll get." He swung back toward the steps. "Let's get out of this light. Come out in the street if you want me to give it to you."

Lyla was shocked at the look of Mark's face.

He didn't say a word, just got up and started walking. Even with a hand caught in the pocket of his coat she had to pretty nearly run to keep up with him. He seemed completely to have forgotten the posse in the creek bottom. The angles of his face were bleak and rigid as granite. She cried, "Muleshoe — don't be a fool!"

His head came around but his eyes went straight through her. His glance swung back toward the lights of the town, but he wasn't seeing them, either. What he saw was in his mind and the reflection of it frightened her.

A kind of sob burst out of him. "First Pop Henshaw," he said with the words creeping through his clenched teeth. "Now Eph and Krieger."

His fists looked like white pieces of bone.

She knew this wild anger was going to have to find an outlet. She reckoned he was going into Blossom to hunt Curly and she was terribly afraid. Not for Curly but for Mark. This town believed Mark a renegade. He'd be faced with the gun of every man who swapped looks with him.

She tried to reason with Mark then, tried to hold him; but he flung her hands away from him and tramped on, glance implacable.

Curly, he imagined, would be expecting him. Not this early perhaps, but he must know Mark surely would be after him if he were able and would have taken whatever precautions he deemed advisable to protect himself.

Mark, considering this, turned into Blossom's street, hearing the hoofs of horses behind him. That would be Fraesfield's posse. He didn't chance giddiness by twisting his head. What strength he had left must be saved up for Curly.

He hadn't guessed a man could be so tuckered, so used in body and spirit that each lift of his foot required a definite effort. Inside the furnace of his head his mind clutched at the glimpse of things deeply felt yet too blurred by pain to be fetched into focus. He had a moment of panic when wagon tracks, preserved in frozen mud unseen beneath this snow, set him stumbling and the hinges of his knees began to give.

He caught himself awkwardly and stood breathing hard, but told her grimly to get back when the girl would have reached to help him. The sound of music ran over the snow and the gleam of lamps flung light, butter yellow, across the swept boards of the hotel porch as some departing cattleman pulled open the door.

A dim pattern of voices drifted out on the heels of the man's booted feet. Mark was about to shove on when the crash of a shot slammed the fronts of the buildings. A frantic cry knifed the echoes. Near the center of the street two men, locked together, swayed into the wedge of light and broke apart, one man falling as the gun roared again. The other sprang toward the porch.

Hurrying shapes converged on the man who had fallen and Mark, unnoticed in this traffic, was swept forward with it. Over the heads of those nearest he saw the man on the porch make a foolhardy dive to intercept the runner as he dashed up the steps. The man's fist lashed out with the glint of metal. The cattleman, reeling, toppled over the railing. The man with the gun swiveled his head, still running, and light from the lobby, as he plunged through the door, struck across his face. "It's Curly Thorpe!" Lyla cried.

The man on the ground was Gunter. Two men were trying to lift him out of the snow and he was cursing through the bloody froth on his lips. "Damn you, let me alone!" he snarled suddenly. "Get me a doctor — get the sheriff!"

There was a horrible stain spreading over his shirtfront and except for the blood on his chin his face was ashen. His eyes were frightened and vengeful and he had both hands squeezed against his chest. He was sobbing and cursing and talking all at once. "Out of his head," someone muttered; and someone else said, "What was that about Thorpe?"

Gunter caught at the name. "That's right!" he cried, twisting out of their grasp, and wrenched up on an elbow. "It was Curly Thorpe gunned me — I lied to you this noon — he give me five hundred bucks to pin that rustlin' on Dawson. Listen — by God, I'm goin' to tell you the truth! That —"

Mark got free of them then and jumped for the steps. He slipped on the top one and fell and got up again, fighting back the wave of dizziness threatening to engulf him. He reeled through the door and scrubbed a hand across his eyes and saw the staring faces of three cowmen in the lobby. All three stood rooted; two of them thrust empty fists above their heads. The clerk, still clutching his precious hair rope, was sprawled on the floor near the foot of the stairs with blood running out of a gash in his forehead.

"Where'd he go?" Mark demanded, and

three pairs of eyes rolled scared looks toward the balcony.

Mark reached for the banister, free hand yanking his gun out. But he stopped before his foot touched the stairs. He turned his face around. "Don't lie to me! Thorpe's got more sense —"

"He figured," Baiden growled, "to cut down the hall and get out through the kitchen but the cook —"

Mark wasn't waiting for the rest of it. He darted up the stairs and was almost to the landing when a gun exploded, kicking splinters from the banister. Mark dropped flat and jerked off his hat. On hands and knees he went up three more steps and heard a board skreak somewhere just above and beyond him.

Flattened down still more he squirmed two steps higher. The next would put his eyes on a level with the balcony. He hesitated, listening, not minded to stop another slug if he could help it. Curly couldn't afford to stand there forever.

But was he standing there?

Suddenly suspicious Mark raised his left hand above the level of the floor. Nothing happened. He got onto his hands and knees again and saw nothing ahead of him but a line of shut doors. The balcony was empty.

In two bounds Mark was onto it, hearing men coming up the stairs from the lobby. Reckoning Curly had fired from one of these rooms he tried to see which of the doors was ajar. Unable, he put his shoulder to the nearest and twisted the knob. The door was locked.

Drawing back to give himself ramming room, he tried to think if he could have heard it had a key just been turned. He was persuaded he would have and, knowing he hadn't, moved on to the next.

This one gave to his grasp. He flung it wide and stood back. When nothing happened he went in. The room was not lighted but enough came from outside to reveal chair and bureau and, beyond the bulk of the bed, a wide open window.

He rushed to the window. It gave onto the street and showed the porch roof below it. Beyond the edge of the roof he saw the faces of horsemen. No one needed to tell him Curly hadn't gone that way.

About to wheel from the window something made him look down again. Then he knew what had bothered him. The sight of those faces, nearly all of them peering upward.

He turned around and saw the boots, with no one in them, beside the door. He

244

twisted his head and stared at the ceiling. There was a roof trap but it was closed. He looked around more carefully and saw the depressions made by feet on the bed's rumpled counterpane.

He thrust his gun back in leather and got upon it himself. Jouncing his weight on the springs he gathered enough momentum to bounce and catch the edge of the roof trap.

Pain splintered through the wound in his side. Nausea swept over him and he almost lost his hold. He didn't think he had the strength to pull himself high enough to shove the hatch back with his head. But somewhere he found it. Somehow he managed to get the top half of him through and to hang there, half in and half out, trembly and sweating while the gabled roof, perilously dipping and heaving, spun like a view hastily snatched from a carrousel.

When you're expecting a bullet to knock you hell west and crooked, time measured in split seconds can seem forever and a day. This was how it seemed to Mark; then he hauled the rest of him through and lay for other split seconds riding out the final stages of his nausea.

The roof swung back into focus and he saw Curly's tracks and then a bare stretch of tin where the snow had slipped away from this red-painted sheeting. Was this then why Curly had not nailed him? Had he gone with that snow? Or was he waiting behind the squat shape of this chimney which came out of the slant a dozen feet ahead of him? Or behind that other which showed thirty feet yonder across the roof's ridgepole?

Even in dry weather there was enough of a cant to this wet sheeting to make travel dangerous. On top of this, Mark knew, it would be impossible to move even two feet across it without betraying his progress. He could not see the street, only the upper portions of those buildings directly across, the top windows of which were now crowded with faces. He could not see beyond the ridgepole, but the roof of the building next in line on Mark's right was perhaps three feet lower and not too far away but what a desperate man might have tried for it. It had a bare place on it right across from the bare patch of this one.

He heard voices in the room he'd just climbed out of, someone calling for a ladder; and, reaching for his gun, he found the leather empty.

His mind went completely blank for a moment and an all-gone feeling got its hooks into his stomach. Then he remembered the pistol he'd thrust into his pocket, the second one he'd got from Howlett, the one he'd picked up off the floor there at Lyla's.

He still had it. He took it out and he cocked it and started forward, maneuvering cautiously across that canted slippery surface while the cold tin crackled with explosions of sound every time he put knee or hand down. He reached the chimney and paused, trying to catch Curly's breathing. When he couldn't he moved again, wedging knee and hip against its top side, disgruntled when he found no one back of it. If Curly were still on this roof he had to be beyond that ridgepole, probably back of the other chimney.

Mark reckoned if he stretched out with his half-numb feet braced against the masonry he'd be able to look over. He couldn't quite, and the tin beneath his weight made such a horrible racket he guessed it would be too risky to try it if he could. He got a hand over the ridgepiece and tried to blow some heat into the fingers holding his pistol. He'd no way of knowing how Curly was fixed for ammunition but, wearing the fellow's shell belt, he didn't imagine he had any loads to waste. He'd used two slugs on Gunter, fired twice at Mark on the stairway. Unless he'd fetched some extras he couldn't have more than two in the cylinder.

This wasn't quite as good as it sounded. For three years hand-running, before he'd gone off to college, Curly'd taken top honors at the Fourth of July shoots. That hadn't been just luck. He'd had to use two for Gunter but they'd been in close quarters, struggling. He'd wasted two on the stairs, but they'd served their purpose, pinning Mark down while he'd got through the roof. He'd be desperate now but three times as careful. He might still get away with it, discredit Gunter's story and thumb his nose at local opinion if he could shut Mark's mouth now once and for all. Two slugs in Curly's pistol would be more than plenty if he could catch Mark exposed to a look down its barrel.

He forced his mind away from Eph, away from Rube and Henshaw. He could not let himself think of Lyla. He might rush Curly, hoping fright or tension would throw his aim off. He didn't believe it would. This left him one other chance, a grave one but he took it.

Using the mortared bricks for leverage, he thrust himself upward with his head out of sight and put the whole of his left arm over the ridgepole, cursing him when Curly laughed, refusing this plain target.

He didn't dare stand up. He couldn't slither along on one arm far, either, so he threw his left leg over the ridgepole, taking this chance even though it was crazy. Curly held his fire and Mark, like a crab, started toward the far chimney. He had to be careful not to straddle the ridgepole lest he put his whole back within range and give Muleshoe's heir the kind of shot he was wanting.

It was awkward, gruelling, terrible labor to cross thirty feet of open roof in that fashion, expecting any moment to feel the smash and rip of lead and having constantly to be ready to shift his weight if Curly hit him; and when it came he was not ready.

He was scarcely ten feet from the chimney, and with his weight still braced on this side of the ridgepole, when the report of Curly's gun hammered its sound across the rooftop. Mark's left thigh felt as though it had been torn from its socket. He had no sense of equilibrium; his whole lower body came loose of its anchorage and only the desperate grab of his right hand kept him from following it into oblivion. That right hand caught the ridgepiece but it cost him his gun.

He heard the thing's clatter as it slid toward the roof's edge. He heard Curly

moving. Jerked his head up and saw him —
handsome face and upper chest, that forward hunching of big shoulders as he came
around the chimney. "Last I had." He
chuckled. "I'll have to make you acquainted
with the barrel," he said pleasantly.

By prodigal inroads on the dregs of his
strength Mark got both elbows hooked over
the rooftree. Curly, smiling, lunged toward
him with his reached-forward hand flashing
down, pistol weighted.

But he'd forgotten the snow. One foot
shot from under him. He grabbed for the
chimney. Frost and heat and now this
dampness had combined with time to crack
the life from the mortar. The bricks came
away in his hand and he vanished. The last
thing Mark heard was his terrified scream.

We hope you have enjoyed this Large Print book. Other Thorndike, Wheeler or Chivers Press Large Print books are available at your library or directly from the publishers.

For more information about current and up-coming titles, please call or write, without obligation, to:

Publisher
Thorndike Press
295 Kennedy Memorial Drive
Waterville, ME   04901
Tel. (800) 223-1244

Or visit our Web site at:
www.gale.com/thorndike
www.gale.com/wheeler

OR

Chivers Large Print
published by BBC Audiobooks Ltd
St James House, The Square
Lower Bristol Road
Bath BA2 3BH
England
Tel. +44(0) 800 136919
email: bbcaudiobooks@bbc.co.uk
www.bbcaudiobooks.co.uk

All our Large Print titles are designed for easy reading, and all our books are made to last.